TURNAROUND

BY
CRAIG SPECTOR

Back in scriptworld Eric stood in the center of the fourth floor of a deserted parking structure, a sleek metal attaché case upright by his leg. He was dressed entirely in black, eyes fixed on the up ramp. He couldn't see Toad or Trina. That was precisely the point.

From the third floor came the hum of engines; Eric stood his ground as two hulking black SUVs gunned up the ramp, heading straight toward him. Some fifty feet away they parted, pulling into opposing parking slots. Eric watched as the doors opened and a dozen swarthy goons stepped out, assuming flanking positions. Then the shotgun door of the second SUV opened, and Tio lumbered out. He was a hulking East Euro heavy in tailored Armani, all thick jowls and stubble and grim Slavic smile, and straight out of central casting.

"Mister Black," he said in a guttural boom. It sounded like Meestah Blahk. "You have my package?"

Eric nudged the attaché; it fell over by his feet, a heavy echo reverberating through the structure. "Got mine?" he answered.

Tio nodded to his crew. One goon produced a black duffel bag and placed it on the ground near Tio; Tio nodded and the goon unzipped it and gave it a hefty push.

The bag slid across the concrete, stopped neatly before Eric. He glanced down and saw thick bundles of cash stuffed inside.

Eric shoved the attaché with one foot; it slid over to Tio, stopped movie-perfect at Tio's feet. Duffel goon knelt down to open the case. No go. "Locked," he said.

Tio scowled, and growled in thick Slavic tongue. "Nee pees deet Black. Don't fuck with me. What's the combination?"

"Three two one," Eric said pleasantly. Tio nodded to the goon, who clicked the combination on the latch. Three... two... one...

The latch popped free. The goon opened the case.

BOOOOOM! Smoke and flame belched forth as the case blew, wounding Tio and killing half his men in a heartbeat as a shockwave wracked the structure and a hail of returning gun fire sent bullets pinging everywhere. The fire reached one of the SUVs, which began to burn.

DEDICATION

For Tess,
My love, my best friend, my wife —
We took the scenic route
but we finally found each other.
Here's to the rest of it, bebe…

ACKNOWLEDGMENTS

Thanks to David Niall Wilson and David Dodd of Crossroad Press, for this new edition;

to my sister Kim Spector and my mom Barbara Spector, for familia;

to my friends old and new, both online and IRL;

Special thanks to my medical team: Dr. Wiley Zhu, Dr. Jody Boggs, Dr. Erik Lappenin, Dr. Douglas Kelly, Dr. Mark Fleming, the EVMS residents, Dr. Hershmerger and Dr. Ouyang, and the awesome Sentara Trauma nursing and caregiving staff, for fighting the good fight to keep me here a little longer;
to Chris, Elise, and Kimberlee at Change Health Care, for helping to keep the wheels turning;

to the fine folks at gofundme.com, and all the contributors to my fundraiser, for helping to make the Resurrection Road a little smoother;

to my attorney L. Wayne Alexander, for always having my back;

and of all, to my beautiful, caring, wonderfully crazy wife, Maria Theresa Ugot, for being the epitome of grace under fire and bringing me more love, joy, and happiness than I ever imagined or probably deserve.

Turnaround, n., 1. *(road), a type of junction which enables traffic heading in one direction to efficiently turn around and head in the opposite direction. Sometimes used as a synonym for cul-de-sac. 2. (music), in jazz or blues, a term referring to a passage at the end of a section, which leads to the next section. 3. (film industry term), the process wherein the rights to a project one studio has developed are sold to another studio in exchange for the cost of development. Often used as jargon meaning the death of a project.*

— Wikipedia.com

ACT ONE

LOS ANGELES, 2010

FADE UP ON:

It was almost midnight when Eric Best screeched the old Nissan 300Z into the empty parking lot at the end of Esplanade and wracked the steering wheel, fat tires squealing as the car whipped around. Headlights illuminated the low blue-stained wooden fence at the edge of the lot as Eric threw open the driver's door and climbed out, the engine still rumbling. He was in his 40s, good looking enough, thinning hair cropped short, one ear pierced, decent bone structure but body starting to thicken… but like the car, they'd both seen better days.

The cold glimmering Pacific churned surf at water's edge before him; the twinkling black rocky hook of the Palos Verdes foothills jutted into the bay some five hundred yards south, past where the flat gray ribbon of bike path ended on the sand; to the north, the sweep of Esplanade as it hugged the beach: pricey apartment buildings and overbuilt condos squeezed up against older single family homes, all lining the inland side, but an obstructed view of expansive beach on the other. He knew this view, all too well — it was his solace as well as his neighborhood, and many a sunset he had come down here to watch the sinking sun kiss the horizon, a Technicolor light show of epic beauty and peace, oft times the only good moment in his day. Clear night like this, he could see the lights all the way to Malibu.

Eric squinted past the edge of the headlights to the deserted lifeguard station below. She wasn't there. Something was wrong. He could feel it, and it filled him with a dull knife pang of dread. Eric speed-dialed his cellphone.

"C'mon, pick up…" he hissed. The call flipped to voicemail: a woman's voice, sunny and chipper.

"Hi, if you want me, you know what to do…. " A throaty laugh. An annoying beeeep.

"Shit!" Eric hung up. In the middle distance he could see the old pier. He jumped back in his car and gunned it down the street: a man on a mission, with a terrible sense it might already be too late.

The pier was old school funky, a series of overlapping triangles next to the little harbor, with bait stations for fishermen on the outer seaward periphery, cheesy souvenir shops, greasy eateries and ice cream stands clustered shoreside. By day it was filled with a mix of upscale yuppies and ethic working class families; at this hour it was largely deserted, though Eric could hear 80's rock and roll thudding from the smattering of dive bars… and under that, the ceaseless drone of pounding surf. It was April, and chilly, and a sudden marine layer of fog had rolled in, misty tendrils clinging to the light posts and hanging in the night air.

Eric moved quickly, eyes darting as he scanned in every direction for some sign. As he cleared the last shop the outer pier opened up, a series of arching steel triangles rising to form a sort of canopy. To his left, the bay and the open ocean; to his right, waves pushed passed massive barnacled pylons, churning toward the rocky strip of inner beach a hundred yards back. He paused and looked down: a faded mural of a jolly whale and happy splashing dolphins was painted on the concrete at his feet. But as he turned back, something caught his glance. Small, inert, out of place. He recognized it.

It was abandoned near a bait table near the railing. A purse. Hers.

"No…". Eric gasped, heart pounding as his stomach fisted its way up his throat. "NO!!

He ran over and peered over the rail into blackness, three-foot waves smashing past pylons that loomed like the legs of dark giants, the water inky and foam flecked. For one mad moment, he saw only sea…

…then her head popped up, gasping for breath in the trough between waves. In other circumstances she would be pretty; at this moment she looked like a drowning cat. Her arms broke surface and flailed as she sputtered. Then another wave hit, and she was under.

Back on the pier, Eric freaked as time both sped up and slowed elastically, a thousand thoughts racing through his mind in a microsecond as he stripped off his jacket and dialed 911 on his cell.

"911, what's your emergency?" the voice on the phone asked.

"There's a woman in the water off the pier!" he yelled. "She jumped!" He looked down and saw her head bob back up between waves; she was conscious, flailing. "SWIM!!" he called out to her. "SWIM with the waves!!"

He watched as she tried. He could hear sirens from the police substation and fire department splitting the night. Then another wave hit, and she went under again.

"Fuck!" Eric dropped the cell, climbed on the rail, and jumped.

And in the ensuing rush of time and careening black space, something odd happened.

Eric plummeted, the height of a two-story building whipping past as the waves rose up. He hit and pierced the water's black surface feet first, sank, fought his way back up through roiling current and system-shocking cold. His head and shoulders broke the surface and he smelled brine, seaweed, the clammy taint of dead fish, the slimy trace of diesel and oil in the water. He had landed close, maybe eight feet away from her.

"Hang on!" he cried, and swam toward her just as her head went face down from shock and exhaustion. Eric grabbed her and flipped her on her back, one arm snaking under her shoulder and around her breasts as he clawed through the water, riding the push of each next wave. He could hear sirens past the roar of the surf; high above, people had come out of the bars and watched from the pier rails...

...and then Time glitched, like some Karmic rewind button on a life tape loop, and he was falling again: Eric felt and saw and smelled the same sensations of the jump, the water, the sinking, unmitigated terror and adrenaline-drenched desperation. He fought his way back to the surface.

"Hang on!" he cried, and a wave filled his mouth, saltwater rocketing up his sinuses. Eric sputtered and flailed, tried to swim toward her, his entire body chilled and numb. And that's when he realized: his feet didn't work. The cold kept him from feeling his ankles, snapped from the impact. As he tried to swim to her his strength failed and he found himself backwashed into the pilings, felt the raw pain of his back as the heavily crusted barnacles shredded his shirt and cheese-gratered his flesh, chewing him up. The wave past and Eric slumped, catching another mouthful of merciless sea, laced with his own blood. Then another wave hit...

...and Eric was falling again. Hitting the water again. Sinking, coming up again. But this time, the cold did it: he was not drunk, and she was, the perverse logic of a severely elevated BAC insulating her from the effects of rapid hypothermia. Eric had no such luck or mercy, and he felt the sting of the surf like ten thousand needles injecting him with oblivion. His body seized up as his nervous system short-circuited, limbs leaden and adrift, throat constricting as his heart pounded mad counterpart to his heaving, oxygen starved lungs. And as she flailed and swam for shore the waves pulled him down, and Eric sank, his last thought a tortured, terrified NO...

And then it was dawn. Chill. Grey. Desolate. Eric stood on the rocks lining the inner beach: alone, unshaven, sunken-eyed. And dry. As it happened, he had never gone into the water, after all.

While she, as it happened, had never come out.

The police and ambos were long gone. The rest of the world was just waking up. A little Harbor Patrol boat putted around the inner waters, dropping a hook on a long line. Searching for the body.

They might find it, he had been told. They might not. It might drift out and south with the currents. Show up in Newport Beach or elsewhere on the Orange County shore, a clump of seaweed wrapped around a pallid surprise. In a week, or a month, or six. Or not at all.

Eric drew a husking breath and hit the replay button on his cellphone. Her last message played, for the thousandth time since, as he held it to his ear.

"Eric I'm so sorry… Forgive me…"

Eric lowered the phone. Croaked a desperate mantra.

"What have I done?" he said. "What have I done?"

SIX WEEKS EARLIER

1.

The computer monitor was sleek and black, a brand new Dell LCD flat panel upon which a browser window showed a woman clad in a studded leather S&M harness, surgically augmented breasts hanging like overripe hydroponic fruit. The woman was nearly naked and kneeling, framed from chin to the taut rise of her hips, all pale skin and blood red lips and dark fat nipples, tiny waist and pierced belly button, radiating wanton sexual excess. Her neck was thrown languorously back, face obscured by a tangle of thick black hair. The image was enlarged until the individual pixels became an oscillating connect-the-dots simulacrum of reality; as her torso thrust up and down a plume of smoke uncoiled from her lips and she moaned an erotic mantra.

I just want to smoke… and fuck… and smoke… and fuck….

Eric leaned forward in his Aeron chair and stared at the screen as another woman came into frame behind the first: this one older, salon tanned, and bleach-blond, snaking black latex-clad arms around the first woman's waist and gliding up across her breasts, a lit cigarette in one hand. As she brought it to those wet red lips the first woman sucked and thrust more deeply, quickening her carnal pace.

I just want to smoke… and fuck… and smoke… and fuck….

Eric watched, sharp eyes dully focused. He'd seen enough. As the digital bims went at it with ersatz abandon he moved his mouse, scrolling the cursor over to the far side of the screen, where a list of search engine terms was displayed for the website HOTSMOKINGSLUTS.COM. Next to each word were checkboxes marked approve or deny. Eric clicked down the list.

FETISH: APPROVE... SMOKING: APPROVE....DILDO: APPROVE... MARLBORO: DENY...

Eric's right hand clicked the mouse again and the digital bims disappeared in mid-smoke 'n' fuck. He leaned back in the chair and pulled off his earbud headphones, surveying his domain: beside and around him some three hundred other intrepid souls pounded out their own tasks in Search Engine Optimization, computer keyboards clicking like plastic Chiclets, counterpointed by the dim tinny din of dozens of iPods playing different songs, snatches of low conversation, the palpable hum of an open hive in full day shift stride.

The room was vast and softly lit in ergonomically perfect permanent twilight, the windows tinted to better to minimize eyestrain; the glow of hundreds of similar monitors pulsed like the lights of a miniature city. The computers were all mid-level state of the art workstations; an ergo expert had come in the morning to measure Eric for his own Aeron and stave off the encroachment of productivity-sapping Carpal Tunnel Syndrome or lower back compression, typical injuries in this line of work. Eric had to admit it wasn't bad as day gigs went, if you were willing to unplug your frontal lobe and just roll with the Zen of it all. But there was still the gnawing discontent of his status as a temp digital wage slave, and happy surface trappings aside the whole thing felt like business casual by Kafka, Orwell with free Starbucks.

Eric hated every bloody second of it. And it was only his first week on the job.

Outside, the LA sun was blindingly bright as Eric stood and smoked, sipping lukewarm dregs of coffee, his tenth of the morning. Before him people hustled in and out of the entrance, yapping into cell phones and keying their crackberries in a ceaseless swarm of energetic commerce. Eric leaned up against the wall near the foyer fountain cum Koi pond and caught a glimpse of himself in the building's smoked glass façade — a 21st century digital peon. He still carried himself with a modicum of hipster style and his face, though careworn, still retained some semblance of the confidence he had felt in his former life. If no one looked too hard or cared too much, which no one did, he could possibly front himself as still in the game, or deep in thought, or at least still amongst the living. But in all Eric felt like a man being slowly squished into the earth by some great unseen weight, the collective tonnage of his failure rattling behind him like the chains of Marley's ghost. He hoped it didn't disturb the Koi.

He pulled out his cell, dialed. The ritual calling of the agent. Load up the call sheet — enough to keep your pin in the ever-shifting map, not so much as to be stalkerish. Too many unreturned calls sent a message.

"Nick Freeman's office..." Nick's assistant, David.

"David, this is Eric Best..." Eric said, thinking like you didn't know, Caller I.D.'s a bitch. "Nick in?"

"I'm sorry, Eric, he's not. I'll tell him you called..."

"Thanks, David." Eric didn't add again to David's practiced response. Bad to sound needy. He rang off.

Eric glanced at his watch, a tanky Diesel bought with residuals off his last movie, a made-for-TV extravaganza about tsunamis hitting a surf competition that he wrote in ten days about a million years ago. It was a total goof to him at the time and the producer hired him because she knew he could deliver in a tight crunch, and the network was racing to slipstream the movie into the buzz between two big budget studio films also, imaginatively enough, about tsunamis. Such was the inbred wisdom of Hollywood, where most projects gestated for ages or died en utero as their better fed kin toddled off to terrorize the megaplexes, killing the minds of millions, one brain cell at a time. Eric had worked with the same producer for three years on adapting his first novel and they still hadn't gotten it made; this turd rocketed through development and into production so fast Eric could only laugh his way to the bank. One more blip on the collective radar, another credit on imdb.com, and a nice chunk of change to fund the greater good of his life.

But that was a long time ago. Old enough to carbon date. Like Eric. And now here he stood: on break from a minimum wage stint as an "SEO Specialist" for one of the lesser search engine companies, with two minutes to go before his next training session.

"HOOYAH!" Eric muttered as he stubbed his smoke and tossed the coffee. He wasn't being ironic; he now worked for HOOYAH!, the company's name etched into the glass of the double doors, the seam neatly bisecting the name between the HOO and the YAH! Eric walked toward his reflection, smiling a thinly veiled grimace. Then the doors hissed open and his reflection parted as he passed through, heading back inside.

The conference room was windowless, walls plastered with dry wipe boards covered in scribbles like cuneiforms of a lost civilization. A series of long tables sat in neat lines; at two dozen chairs sat Eric and the other temps, each with their thick three-ring company binders, each one emblazoned with the company logo and the words SEO: SEARCH ENGINE OPTIMIZATION. They were a diversity wet dream mix of early twenties to late forties, male and female, every race and demographic. Most were dressed like Eric, in careful business casual; a few older male hopefuls were clad in cheap suits, projecting awkward downward mobility. Eric sat in the front row, the better to take it all in.

A pretty thirtyish woman, Jennifer, was their training supervisor: neat blonde hair pulled back, navy blazer pantsuit, tasteful jewelry. She looked over her group and smiled.

"So how is everyone liking their first week?" she asked.

Eric and everyone answered in mock confident assent. "Great... love it... no problem..."

Jennifer beamed. "Great!" she said. "I know it's trickier than it looks, but you'll get the hang of it. HOOYAH! thrives because we understand that the advertisers depend on us to lead them to their sites... and we depend on all of you!"

She singled out one temp, a dredlocked mom in Ross markdown dress for success. "How many did you get today?" Jennifer asked.

"Three hundred forty?" the woman replied.

"Great," Jennifer smiled and turned to another temp, a downsized mid-management suit. "And you...?"

"Four hundred twelve…" the man replied. Jennifer beamed and pointed at Eric, glancing down to catch his nametag.

"How about you, Eric?"

Eric glanced down at his tally sheet. "Um, six hundred ninety two…" he said.

Jennifer took it all in. "The average SEO Specialist can process two thousand terms per shift." She watched as the room visibly deflated, then smiled again. "But don't worry, you'll get there! Just study your book, and have fun!"

Jennifer held out her hands, ushering everyone to rise. They did and met her in the center aisle, forming a rough circle. Following her lead, everyone placed their hands in the huddle.

"Okay, on three…" she said. "One… two… three…!"

Everyone chimed in unison.

"Hoooo… YAHHH!!"

2.

The name on the door under the sign for the California Wellness Center read GABRIEL LOEHMAN M.D.. Eric was inside the little West Side office, doing his customary forty-five minute angst-o-rama, the ritual disgorging of his bi-weekly round of soul bile. Trying to level it off just enough to not leak onto the carpet.

"So how's the new job?" Gabe asked, sitting back in his chair and sipping a coffee.

"Fabulous," Eric said. "It's a silicon sweatshop where every keystroke is monitored and every human resource squeezed to the last bloody drop, and I want to gnaw off my own arms to get out of there. But the coffee's good."

Gabe smiled; he was in his fifties, bespectacled and genial, and as shrinks went Eric found him refreshingly un-shrinky — their sessions were less therapy than a running mutual dialogue on the absurdity of life. When Eric's WGA health coverage had run out Gabe had gone sliding scale, charging him twenty bucks a session; when even that became problematic Gabe just let it slide altogether. "And you and Paige?" he asked.

"Um, let's see," Eric began. "She was up my ass when I wasn't working and now she's up my ass because it isn't good enough..."

Gabe nodded ruefully as Eric continued. "I keep telling her it's not like I'm turning down all these fabulous opportunities — it took me nine months to even find this, and I'm a fucking temp! The economy sucks and it feels like after everything I've done I'm pretty much unemployable."

"And she resents that..." Gabe said.

"Not that. Me," Eric said flatly. "Me, of course, I'm thrilled."

Eric sighed and leaned back in his chair, his legs splaying out. "I had to convert my credit list into a résumé, right?" he said. "Okay fine, I can do that — hell, I rewrote résumés for her and half her friends. But how do you explain why you haven't had a straight job in twenty years? It's easier to tell an interviewer I was in prison than try to explain what I've done with my life."

"But you did a lot," Gabe countered.

"And where is it now?" Eric laughed ruefully. "That's what Paige always comes back to. Look where it got me. It's like it actually counts against me. I went for a position as a copywriter with an ad agency. This human resources dweeb looked me right in the eye and said, you're too old. Like, seriously?"

"Human resources," Gabe smiled. "That term always gets me. Like they're actually interested in humans."

"Oh they're interested," Eric said. "Interested in carving people up for parts to feed into the corporate Borg. I remember when I was in high school the government reinstituted the draft registration. Not the draft, just the registering part."

Gabe nodded; he was a full-on Boomer and remembered it well. "I had just missed the cutoff age by six months, right?" Eric continued, "And I saw this political cartoon with this herd of cows and this guy was drawing dotted lines on their torsos. One cow looks at the other and says, don't worry they just want to know how much meat is available."

Gabe chuckled. Eric just shook his head. "I've done my share of shit work," he said. "Drove trucks, worked warehouse, security guard, dishwasher, crawled under fucking trailers installing cable TV. When I was in college I worked graveyard at the old Boston Herald, just me and fifty tons of newsprint and a couple of hundred rats. It's not about that...

"But how do you explain to a supervisor who's sitting there dreaming of one day quitting their shitty job one day to write their big novel or screenplay that you want to crawl back into their world? I feel like, and here I sit, the death of your motherfucking dream..."

Eric leaned forward, head resting on his hands, staring into some inner abyss. Gabe switched gears.

"What about that new project you were talking about?"

"Still in development hell," Eric said. "Marty wants more rewrites. Just doesn't wanna pay for 'em."

Gabe nodded; he had a number of industry clients and the story was commonplace, especially after the big Writers Guild Strike of '08-09. Working in film meant working with Guild writers, at least at a studio or network level; the rules were clear. But everyone knew you had to do what you had to do to get a project greenlit, so secret courtesy drafts were standard issue. Small stuff: a tweak here or there to fine-tune things, like getting your car detailed. Somewhere along the way the courtesy became an expectation, and the expectation became an unspoken requirement, just as the range of what was required expanded to full-blown page one rewrite and re-defining the entire concept. Somewhat akin to taking your Camry into a carwash and expecting a Maserati to come out the other end.

It was totally against the rules and if a signatory company got busted for it the Guild would come back hard on the writer's side, but they'd only know if the writer reported them. Which was a great way to never work again.

"I don't know," Eric sighed grievously. "I don't want to be a pussy about this. I never expected any of this to be easy. But does it have to be this goddamned hard?"

Gabe just nodded and smiled, but Eric wasn't. "I keep trying to think my way out of this," he said. "But it's like my thoughts are running in these little toxic circles, like a rabid hamster wheel in my head. I keep telling myself if I just go deeper I'll find the answer. But I don't see a good end to any of it anymore."

"Any of what?" Gabe asked.

"It. Me. My stupid fucking life," Eric said.

Silence. Gabe thought for a moment, then sat up in his chair. "I want to you to try something," he said, reaching into his desk drawer and handing Eric some crinkly foil-backed plastic packets. Eric squinted at the label, the drug's name rendered in flowing baby blue type.

"Synethstra?" he said skeptically.

"Next generation of SNRI," Gabe explained. "Basically a new class of serotonin-neoepinephrene uptake inhibitor. It's powerful but subtle, fast acting. Just to level out your brain chemistry a bit."

"I dunno, Gabe," Eric said warily. "I'm kinda not into the better living through chemistry thing?"

"Except for caffeine, nicotine and alcohol?" Gabe shot back.

"Those are food groups, though," Eric conceded. Gabe smiled. Bastard knew him too well.

Gabe stood and waxed serious. "Neurotransmitter proteins are kind of like oil in your brain's engine," he said as he took out his Rx pad and scribbled. "Extended periods of extreme stress burn them off. I think you qualify."

"So you're saying my mental dipstick is dry?" Eric said, getting up.

Gabe handed him the scrip. "One a day, with food. Watch your alcohol intake, get rest, and quit smoking already, will ya, guy?" he chided. "You have any problems, let me know."

"Anal leakage," Eric mumbled. "Erections lasting more than four hours..."

"That last one would be a high class problem," Gabe said.

Eric hit the street and lit a smoke, looking at the sample packets Gabe had given him. Synethstra, 20 mg. He sighed. He had to get home, unpack. Make dinner. Write. He had another notes meeting with Marty tomorrow afternoon.

Eric popped a tab out of the packet and swallowed it.

What the hell, he thought. Any port in a storm....

3.

The 405 was a winding eight-lane traffic jam as Eric crawled along, heading south. His cellphone rang; the Caller I.D. said NICK. A call from his agent. Miracle. Eric keyed on, rolling up his window, the better to enjoy his non-functioning A/C.

"Nick," Eric said.

"Eric, how's my favorite writer?" Eric glanced over and saw the Century City skyline, could picture Nick, a sleek and effete heatseeker, leaning back in his desk chair, gazing out the high-rise windows.

"Broke, Nick," Eric replied. "You gotta squeeze Marty's nuts a little... he needs to pay me." Eric pictured Nick, rolling his eyes.

"No can do, buddy, believe me, I tried. You're the only writer on this one Eric, and Marty likes you. It's gonna open a lot of doors for you if you deliver for him."

"I've already delivered!" Eric's turn to roll his eyes. "How much more?"

"Home stretch, buddy. You just got to hang in a little longer. Make him happy."

"Right..." Eric sighed.

4.

Eric pulled up in front of the Seascape Apartments, backing his car into a curbside slot. The car was a shadow of its former self. Eric had bought it years back on a whim, his reward for being tortured by a thriller he had worked on about a burned out tattoo artist to the stars and a serial killer collecting human pelts of her work. It was arguably an intriguing idea at the time and was also one of the easiest gigs he had ever scored — one chattily intense lunch meeting and Eric was hired.

It was only afterwards that the migraines set in — endless meetings trying to beat out the outline with execs who could not decide what they wanted but knew whatever it was Eric had just come up with wasn't it; endless drafts trying to flesh out the character and give her the requisite darkness and torment only to have it scraped off in the next notes meeting. When Eric had spotted the Z on a South Bay lot he bought it on the spot. Maybe it was his middle class upbringing or middlebrow tastes but Eric had never cared about the Beamers, Mercs or Porsches that were the wet dreams of upward thrusting industry types, or the Ferraris, Bentleys and Hummers of the stupidly rich and grossly indulgent. He just liked what he liked and thought the Z was cool — a sleek silver sportster, low and lean with lines like a shark. It was used with low miles, had a flawless leather interior and Bose sound system, T-tops and a twin turbo, it was destined to be a classic and had been pre-owned by some Asian doctor's wife who must not have weighed enough to crease the driver's seat. Eric happily drove it away thinking, hate this project... love this car, and had babied it for years.

The movie never got made. Now the car's paint was faded

and it leaked fluids; the driver's side door handle was broken and Eric couldn't afford to fix it, the tranny was slipping and he couldn't fix that either. And God help him when the head gasket blew, which he knew it was soon to do. He popped the hatch and pulled out a heavy cardboard moving box marked SCRIPTS, hauling it into the complex.

The Seascape was a tidy little courtyard building some three blocks from the beach, nestled on a hill in the Avenues just off Palos Verdes Blvd. Couldn't see the ocean but you could smell it. The building itself was circa 1950s and originally housed personnel from a nearby military base; it was later converted to private units and recently renovated with granite counters, new cabinets and appliances, Berber carpet and ceiling fans, the better to jack the rents and lure in higher-paying tenants. But the beach chairs by the other units' doors signaled that this was perhaps more of a community than the faceless Pasadena yuppie warren Eric and Paige had previously called home, which had condo'ed out from under them at exactly the wrong time in Eric's downward career trajectory and added another twelve tons of emotional debris to their marital discord.

And the layout of the courtyard, with all the units facing inward, was such that one might actually get to meet one's neighbors, if one wanted to. Their unit, number 35, was cool and airy, and the courtyard had the kitschy charm of a funky beach hang. When Eric and Paige had first seen the lush tropical vegetation and little kidney-shaped pool he felt a sense of ease, like this might be a good place to live, to write. To rebuild his career, and maybe even their life together.

"Hi neighbor!" Eric heard a cheery voice and looked up to see Marin and Bob, two of the friendlier denizens, sitting at their customary perch at top of the stairs and taking in the evening air.

"Hey Marin... Bob..." Eric said, pausing and putting down the box. Bob looked over and smiled a squinty smile, nodded yo.

"Still moving in?" Karen enquired. "Wow you guys have a lot of stuff..."

"This is the last of it," Eric explained.

"Yeah," Marin nodded knowledgably. Bob squinted and said, "Man, I hate moving."

Marin stood and shifted in her fuzzy slippers, tossing back long auburn hair. Eric had met them as he first moved in three weeks ago and every night since. They were a twenty-something slacker couple who lived in the first unit on the second floor, one of the few remaining "pre-models", not yet renovated, and they had been there for years. Bob was a marginally employed, emotionally stunted surfer stoner while Marin held sway as the reigning worker's comp queen of the courtyard, chain-smoking and sipping box wine as she continually kvetched about her back injury from once working at Trader Joe's. Eric found them alternately amusing, eccentric, and vaguely irritating.

"How's your back?" Eric asked.

"Oh you know," Marin said, "they're still jerking me around on my surgery." Eric nodded; in the last three weeks he'd heard about it maybe twenty times. "Hey!" She brightened. "I met your wife... Patty?"

"Paige," Eric corrected.

"Right, Paige," Marin said. "I'm terrible with names. Never forget a face though. She's really pretty. What does she do?"

"She works at a big firm downtown," Eric said, then added, "I usually work at home."

"Oh really?" Marin chirped. She lived for this kind of info. "What do you do?"

"I'm a writer," Eric explained, "though lately I've been doing some consulting for an Internet company." As lies went it was palatable and marginally face-saving, and judging from Marin's nodding acceptance it worked just fine.

"I wondered!" she said. "What kind of stuff?"

"Movies, TV," Eric said. "Horror, thrillers, anything twisted or sick."

"Wow," Marin said. "I see the lights on in your place at night and it looked kinda creepy. I told Bob, what does he do? Didn't I Bob?"

"Yup," Bob nodded.

"Anything I might have seen?"

"Maybe," Eric replied. He always hated that question. How

the hell did he know what she might have seen? "Had a couple of movies made, did one of the Frightmare! movies."

The Frightmare! reference piqued their interest, not the 1974 Peter Walker film but a later and hugely successful franchise about a crazed maniac clown who had died in a vigilante acid bath and his mutilated undead spirit came back to kill teenagers in their dreams. The original was a low budget box office surprise and scary as hell, but as it took off the series eventually winnowed down to the horror equivalent of Count Chocula as the studio strip-mined every last ounce of cash off the concept.

Eric had done one of the latter sequels, Frightmare 9!: The Dream Tool. Got the gig by pitching a new twist on the mythos hinging on the Jungian collective unconscious and how the inner doorways of perception could swing both ways, allowing the heroine to enter the madman's dreams to defeat him. Eric did the first draft, and seven other writers later it became somewhat less than that. Something about an amusement park and a killer baby.

But the brand name still had flash cred: Frightmare! was a theme park ride now, and even the most baked halfwit could invoke the trademark cackle of the clown killer, one of the only lines of Eric's contribution that survived the final cut. Which Bob now spontaneously did.

BWOOhahahh are we having FUN yet???," he croaked, cocking his head toward Eric, who smiled and looked away. "Cool, you wrote that?"

"Yeah," Eric said, less fake humble then vaguely embarrassed. "A while ago."

"Whoa, so you're sorta famous!" Bob said.

"Yeah," Eric smiled and chuckled a sigh. "Sorta."

5.

It was almost seven thirty when Paige came home from work. Eric had busied himself unpacking boxes, cleaning the kitchen, and starting to cook dinner. His culinary expertise was utilitarian at best: grilled chicken, rice, sautéed vegetables. It wasn't that he totally sucked at it but rather that he did it without any real love for the task; food was fuel best served simple and when deep in deadline Eric often forgot to even eat. Paige on the other hand was the better cook but a fairly terrible housekeeper; in the earlier days of their marriage the duties divided along relatively easy lines — Paige cooked, went to school and worked retail; Eric cleaned the apartment, made the bed, did laundry, maintained the cars, took out the trash, and tended to all other and sundry "manly" tasks, i.e., anything too onerous or disgusting for Paige to want to deal with... and paid most of the bills, as he wrote fulltime to support them both. The domestic disparity wasn't something he had dwelled upon — he had lived on his own for years before they met, and had to do it all anyway when he was a divorced bachelor. But as the power balance shifted, it did start to grind.

And shift it did — as fate would have it, Paige's graduation from UCLA in the fifth year of their union marked the ascent of her personal career star just as Eric's began its seemingly inexorable and meteoric descent. Her first real job at a South Bay firm brought the mix from roughly ten percent of their household earnings to thirty in the space of a year, just as his began sliding downward; two years later she jumped to a bigger downtown firm, with a concurrent salary bump that made them fifty-fifty, and the year after that she took the lead. It made neither of them happy, though as it turned out for completely different reasons.

"Hey hon," Eric said as Paige came through the front door and set down her heavy leather attaché.

"Hi." Paige hung her Pashmina scarf on the rack behind the door and then went over to put her Blackberry in the charger on the desk. Three weeks in and their new home look almost settled within the first four days; Eric was good at moving and had done pretty much all of it himself, hauling a load a day in Paige's old 4Runner and unpacking each room as he moved it, then getting a U-Haul for the big stuff. By the time he was done the new place already looked lived in; only his office in the second bedroom was left to fine-tune. Eric came around the counter and they exchanged a perfunctory kiss.

"How was your day?" he asked.

"All right," she said. "What's for dinner?" She looked at what was on the stove, gave a little shrug that either meant okay or oh god not again, and headed off to the bedroom to change her clothes. Eric put the food on the big pine table just off the narrow kitchen, uncorked a bottle of Two Buck Chuck for her and grabbed himself another beer as Paige came back in, dressed in comfy sweats, brown hair pulled loosely back and held with a couple of hand-painted chopsticks. She still had her makeup on. She was a pretty woman, slender and meticulously accessorized at all times, but her features were starting to take on the distinctively downward tilt of someone deeply dissatisfied with life. Her own, certainly. But more so, his.

They sat down to eat; Paige riffled absently through the mail, their silence punctuated by an episode of Law & Order playing low and unwatched on a Visio plasma on the living room hutch. "I got you a present today," she said. Eric looked at her and Paige continued, "I put you on my life insurance policy at work."

"Wow," Eric said, thinking *how romantic.* "Thanks."

"Well I need some kind of security," Paige said. "God knows you're not getting any younger."

"No, it makes sense," Eric agreed. "That's fine. How much?"

"A half million dollars," she said. "I would have gotten more but you're over forty and you smoke."

"I'm worth more dead than alive," Eric muttered jokingly.

Paige was not amused. She finished eating, pushed the picked over plate away, poured some more wine, and lit a cigarette of her own from his pack on the table. Paige was a social smoker, usually at parties or when she was having a glass of wine, but when she lit up at home Eric instinctively braced himself.

"How is the job?" she asked.

"It's all right I guess," Eric said, trying to, if not muster enthusiasm, at least not paint a fresh laser-dot on his own forehead. "The supervisor keeps saying they're going to hire someone full-time out of my group."

"Well you should go for it, it's better than nothing," Paige replied. She knew full well that if that happened he'd make twice what he did now and less than half what she did, if even, but still. "When will you know?"

"When they decide, I guess," Eric told her, getting up and squeezing past her to grab another beer from the fridge. "I'm not exactly on a need-to-know basis."

"What's that supposed to mean?"

"Nothing," Eric said, feeling the conversational gears shift. "It's just that they don't exactly tell the temps when they're going to do what they're going to do. It keeps us motivated."

"You're not motivated?"

"I didn't say that," Eric defended. "I'm there to do a job so I'm doing a good job at it, but it's not like I love the fact that I'm there in the first place!"

"Well how do you think I feel?" Paige said. "I need some help around here!"

Eric cleared away the plates, rinsing and loading them into the dishwasher. He knew that neither prior support nor current domestic duties counted toward her principal concern, which he all too keenly shared. On the TV, Detective Lenny Brisco was cracking the case; Eric vaguely wondered if when he was done Lenny might solve the caper of Eric's murdered career. Paige went back to riffling mail, pulled out her laptop and started paying bills online.

"What's going with your project?" she asked. He knew what she was really asking, which she then did. "Is he going to pay you yet?"

Eric sighed. "Meeting with Marty tomorrow," he said. "I'll know more then."

"Uh-huh," she said. "Like you did with the movie option?

"That's not fair," Eric said. As he loaded the washer he flashed on the original meeting for his project; he hadn't worked with Martin Blumenthal in several years but then Martin called Eric, asking about the availability of the rights. They met for lunch in Chinatown, Martin talking of his passion for the material and picking up the tab, and on the ride home Eric felt cautiously elated: a lunch like that meant a deal and he was waiting for the callback from his agent to discuss terms. On the way out Martin had graciously offered to order something to take home for Eric's wife but Eric had declined; later Eric had mixed his leftovers into that evening's stir fry, and Paige had noted it was unusually tasty for something he had made.

The call came as they chatted furtively about what the option might be, upfront money which could range from a couple of thousand to five-figures or more, against a six-figure purchase price; they felt a guarded optimism buoyed by a sense that their long storm may have finally passed. Then the phone rang. Paige had watched as Eric listened and left the room, the blood slowly draining out of him. When he came back she asked, what did he say what's the option?

Eric had nodded to her plate. *You're eating it,* he told her.

The lunch was the option. Welcome to the new normal...

"Not fair??" Paige said, plainly affronted. "I work like a dog all day!"

"It's your career," Eric countered. "You're doing what you want to do, you love it there, they love you! But what, when my movie sells you won't work as hard? You'll quit? Stay home and bake cookies?"

"You chose this!" Paige said angrily. "What choice do I have?"

Eric bit back his anger, thought what choice do any of us have babe? All the choice in the world. It was deeply ironic to him that for the first years of their marriage they had never fought, only to later realize their wedded bliss neatly coincided with his ever-expanding ability to provide. She had tanked the LSATS and been turned down for law school twice but it was in her blood: over the last few years of escalating estrangement Eric had come to realize that Paige had subconsciously redlined their vows until she had promised to love, honor and cherish only for richer... for better... in health.

"You have the choice to not make a hard thing worse," Eric told her.

"Yeah right," she said. "You just don't want to deal with reality!"

"What the hell does that mean?" Eric asked.

"Nobody else lives like this!" she cried.

"EVERYBODY lives like this!!" Eric cried louder and tossed his emptied beer in the trash, grabbing another and closing the fridge door just a tad too hard. "Christ, Paige, the whole goddamned country lives like this! You think people who have regular jobs don't worry about losing them?"

He was pacing now, trying to level himself as Paige sat in her chair in the eye of the emotional storm. She finished the glass of wine, got another, then lit another smoke. "I think when normal people lose their jobs they get another one," she said. "They don't sit around feeling sorry for themselves."

"And I'm doing... what?" Eric said sarcastically. "I've got one project out there, I'm always looking for new ones, and now I work this stupid day gig...."

"Yeah, right," Paige huffed. "I made more when I was in school."

"I know," he said. "I was supporting you."

Eric winced even as he said it. Low blows time. If Paige cared she didn't show it; she was on a roll now.

"Uh-huh," she snorted. "Big famous writer. Big movie deal coming. "

"Jesus!" Eric said, his gaze piercing her. "Do you know what it's like to be better at what you do than you've ever been and be worth less for it? To see people who weren't even born when you started get jobs instead of you? Do you know what's it like to live with that?"

"I don't want to live with that!" Paige said. "It's not normal!"

"Well neither am I!" Eric hissed. "When did I ever say I was?"

"That's just your ego and selfishness," Paige countered bitterly. "You don't want to be a man, you don't want to take care of your family! We can't buy a house, we can't plan for our future, we can't do anything! I deserve better than this!"

"Well like Clint Eastwood said," Eric muttered, voice dropping low. "Deserve's got nothin' to do with it."

Perhaps the wrong time to quote Unforgiven. Paige was crying now, valid frustration and self-serving indignation swirling behind her eyes and leaking out to blur her mascara. She looked at Eric, her wide eyes rendered almost clownish, but for the pain.

And then she spoke again.

It was a terrible thing when the one you loved could take your worst and innermost unspoken fear, fashion it a finely honed point, and stab you deep in the heart with it. But they were in combat now, as they had been so many times before. Their verbal thrust and parry were refined by practice and consecrated by time, and Eric had seen and heard and felt them all too many times before. But he had never heard this.

"You have officially ruined my life," Paige said, flat and matter-of-fact.

It stopped Eric dead in his tracks. He looked at her.

"Are you serious?"

"Yes," she said. She wasn't looking at him anymore. She repeated, "You have officially ruined my life."

Eric paused, feeling something buckle in his chest — some deep psychological strut cracked and gave way. He nodded.

"Okay," he said quietly. "And you have officially broken my heart."

Paige said nothing. Then she got up and left the room.

An hour or so later, Paige came back out. The living room blinds were pulled back; the room was dark save for the glow of the TV and the soft lights from the courtyard outside the picture window. Over the roofline of the building the lights of the Palos

Verdes foothills twinkled, distant and serene.

Eric was sitting in the darkness at the kitchen table, a shadow quietly thinking. The kitchen had magically cleaned itself in her absence, as it always did. And he still had to write tonight.

Paige came up, almost as if to apologize. But instead she said something softly, shadowed in the dark.

"When are you just going to admit it's over for you?"

The question hung in the air like stale smoke. Eric stood and looked in her eyes, the darkness masking deep and irretrievable sadness in his own.

"Never," he said.

6.

A lone in the second bedroom, Eric unpacked the box marked SCRIPTS and neatly put them up on the low bookshelf in front of the windows. Atop the bookshelf was a glowing green plasma light, a flat glass disc shooting little bolts of electricity across its surface like something out of Frankenstein's lab. That must be what Marin was talking about, he thought.

The placement of the shelf was part aesthetic, part strategic: it allowed fresh air to circulate but also obstructed the view from outside when he was seated at his desk, and without unduly restricting his own. The net effect was Eric could see out better than others could see in, and a partial view of the L-shaped second floor walkway was possible just by turning in his chair, a full view by simply standing at his desk.

Beneath the shelf he laid neat stacks of his scripts, sorted by project —the titles written in black Sharpie on spines along with the dates. Some had been produced, most labored in development hell before seizing up and never seeing the light of day. The time spans ranged from six months to as many as twenty-six on one project, the latter of which then went on to four or five other writers and, last Eric heard, was still rumored to be going into production one day. They were his cumulative life experience carved up for parts and rendered in twisted fable and fantasy, vivid nightmares and allegorical excoriations of the human condition, the collected body of his work laid out like a tiny morgue slab, or a private museum.

Eric turned off the overhead light and let the night seep in; the mad scientist lamp made things skitter and shift, as if they were alive. It was quiet outside and the sound of the ocean was distant but soothing. He could see the lights from the hills over the roofline; just then he heard something and saw Bob stumbling out to join Marin at the head of the stairs, trying to be quiet but holding on to the railing as if the building were sinking, which was per usual for a weeknight past eleven. Then Bob called back something in the general direction of Eric's window and Eric stepped back into the shadows. He looked past the other side of the shelf and saw who Bob was talking to.

His next door neighbor was coming home. She was tall and gamine, blonde and quite beautiful, though judging from her body language probably a little tipsy, and from her attire probably coming home from a night out. Her front door, Unit 34, was immediately down the three stairs at the end of his unit and maybe thirty feet away, right at the angle of the corner; if he stood by the window it was not so much that he could see it but rather that he couldn't not see it. Eric had glimpsed her several times since he moved in, always coming or going, but they'd never met, and he noticed her the way he always noticed beauty — instinctively but without agenda. Eric lingered, watching as she came to the door and leaned forward, shoulder length hair falling soft and thick to obscure her profile, her long fingers fiddling with her keys.

"Yo KATE!" Bob called out drunkenly until Marin hushed him.

Kate looked in Bob's direction and laughed. She said something back that Eric couldn't hear, but the sound of her laughter was delightful — throaty but sweet, almost girlish. In that moment her head swept around the other way, and Eric stole a glance at her face: blue eyes and wide radiant smile, sensual yet frankly adorable.

She seemed to pause a beat as if sensing him watching. Then the keys clicked and her door opened, and his neighbor stepped inside.

Eric sighed and turned back to the task still at hand, focusing as he turned his attention to his desk. It was big and oak and looked like the bottom half of a roll top, and atop it sat a sleek laptop connected to a large LCD monitor, surrounded by assorted backup drives, hubs and wires, punctuated by winking blue LEDs. It was the centerpiece of his lair and a silicon extension of his brain, his own little digital nerve center, and as Eric fired everything up his thoughts churned back to tonight. Paige was asleep in the bedroom just down the hall mere yards away, but their emotional distance could be measured in light years. The fight adjourned, they had returned to their respective corners — she to sleep and he to pace and burn, his mind smoldering. He got a mad flash of The Exorcist, the quiet before the final storm as the priests ascended the stairs to save Regan's pea-soup spewing soul; young Karras telling the wizened Merrin how he thinks he should bring him up to speed on the phenomena, she seems to exhibit several distinct personalities... and Merrin stopping him, saying There is only one...

Their fights were like that. There was only the one über mega meta-battle submerging and surfacing again and again like some prehistoric creature, each time whipped harder by frustration and the steady attrition of hope. Eric felt wired and resentful and dead inside, pulse pounding in his throat, innards twisted into a tight little fists. As the computer chimed and the desktop mounted Eric opened a desk drawer, pulled out a slim flash drive and plugged it into the hub — extra file backup in case of earthquake or other disaster. The little packets from Gabe where there in the drawer, too, and tucked back in the corner of the drawer was a sinister black shape: a blocky Llama nine millimeter. Fully loaded home defense, a tool for a job one would never want to do.

Eric picked up the gun. It had other uses too, like for another equally unpleasant task. He closed his eyes and felt its heft in his hand, felt the cool hard ring of the muzzle as it slid up to his temple... then to his forehead... then to just under his chin. Then he remembered a video clip of a Pennsylvania politician who had been busted in some forgotten scandal — garden variety graft, corruption, his pudgy hand caught in the commonwealth cookie jar — who then blew his brains out at a live television press conference. Not like in the movies, no gruesome slo-mo skull confetti, just a loud pop as he stuck the gun in his mouth and squeezed the trigger, followed by a torrent of blood and brain matter evacuating from his nose and mouth as his flaccid body dropped like a wet sack drenched in cranial Niagara, as the onlookers all screamed and scrambled…

Eric turned the gun and placed it to his heart. If he held it just so he could squeeze the trigger with his thumb. Just make a fist and boom. Problems solved.

Eric breathed hard, hyperventilating, and glanced toward the window. He had written this before. He had read forensic texts and gone to morgues to stare into the faces of the dead, to try to glean something from their vacant milky eyes, so he could imagine the moment more fully to render on the page. But the dead told him nothing, so in the end he made it up. Imagining. Trying to feel the end in forward tense.

Eric held his breath and tried to squeeze. Nothing. Somewhere in the synaptic relay from brain to hand the message cancelled out. He just couldn't make himself do it. Eric sighed and put the gun back in the drawer, then popped another of Gabe's meds.

His computer chimed; he had new mail. His email was like his phone these days, bearing vexing news or no news at all. He scrolled and deleted the countless Discount Viagra and debt free credit spams, the fun-filled Your Dream Vacation Awaits! pitches and sunny horoscopes, the alert notices that his Visa payment was due. Finally he came to a message from Todd, Martin Blumenthal's young assistant. It read:

Eric — sorry have 2 bump tomorrow's meeting; Marty in Japan, back Sun.. Next Monday at 2? Thx
Todd

The news was both aggravation and reprieve: he wasn't done with the latest notes and could use the extra time. But he knew Paige would shit. It was always like that, first with major letdowns then radiating out to include to the slightest setback, her two first responses to any adverse revelation being oh that's just great! and I knew this was going to happen! In exactly that order.

Eric opened the script doc and scrolled, as the title page filled the screen.

TURNAROUND

Screenplay By

ERIC BEST

Eric scrolled further and started to read, letting the flow of what he had written lead him to the jump off point of what he had to do next, like a runner getting a head start before diving off a cliff. He lit a cigarette and turned on the fan, glancing at his notes scrawled on the printout of the previous draft. One scene header was circled twice.

The note read, Change location — can't afford it!

Painless enough, Eric thought. Ah the joys of pre-production — as they inched ever nearer to moving things from page to screen certain realities came into play, and a script whose eyes were bigger than its budget would not see its light turn green. The INT. PENTHOUSE that was the original home for Eric's lead had proven too pricey as a location, especially since the story called for it to be firebombed toward the end of Act Two.

No problem, though: Marty had a new location lined up. Eric called file images up on the bigger monitor, perused the jpegs from the location scout. He tapped the keys of his laptop, did a global Find/Change, and INT. PENTHOUSE became INT. BEACH HOUSE. Eric started to re-write in the script:

INT. BEACH HOUSE — PRE-DAWN

Chilly. Dark. Quiet. The Pacific thrums in the b.g., the surf visible thru floor-to-ceiling smoke tint, last vestiges of moon breaking thru obsidian clouds. MATT BLACK catnaps on the low bed, his taut form slung across expensive covers, one foot grazing the hardwood floor.

Eric looked at the clock and concentrated, trying to squeeze out all awareness of his surroundings. That he was dog-tired, sleep deprived, stressed out and buzzed was of no consequence; he had to push back the anxiety and self loathing and endless what ifs of his life to will himself into this world, focus on image and character and flow of language until the edges disappeared and nothing else mattered, and he was just in it. The keys clicked. The minutes ticked into hours.

And Eric wrote deep into the night.

7.

He came to consciousness by degrees; slithering up from black slumber like a man emerging from a soft dark cocoon — awareness absent identity first, as gossamer shards of the dream tore and fluttered away. The first glimmer of thought said simply I AM, followed by a moment of searching until a name attached, becoming I AM ERIC. A slight tingling sensation prickled his skin, and in his ears a dull pulsing sound, familiar but too loud, as the thought completed itself.

I AM ERIC BEST.

Eric opened sleep-crusted eyes, his vision blurred and halting. His head pounded with the mother of all headaches. He closed his eyes again.

"Oh shit," he croaked. "Oh Christ..."

He tried to lay still, feeling his intestines do a Cuisinart squirm — afraid to move for fear of disturbing the fragile balance. He could sense the dim intrusion of sunlight behind his lidded eyes, and his senses all felt poised on overload. But just as the pounding in his skull began to recede another force summoned up from his guts, and Eric knew he was destined to hurl. He lurched up and staggered to the bathroom by Braille, retching and coughing. But puke he did not, merely gasping and snarfing for a dreadful beat before turning on the sink and letting the water thunder into the basin. Eric splashed his face and opened his eyes again, waiting for them to figure out how to focus.

"Aw man," he mumbled, blearily thinking christ all nighters I'm getting too old for this shit. Then his eyes focused, and something seemed very wrong.

"What the…?" Eric looked down. The six-pack he had consumed last night was replaced by a six-pack he hadn't seen in years — the one at his waist. Eric blinked, blinked again, reaching through the unbuttoned cotton shirt to feel a set of tanned and rock hard abs. His.

Eric twisted this way and that, looking for love handles which had likewise inexplicably absconded. His body by Budweiser was simply not there; in its place was a Bowflex wet dream, all lean and limber. Eric's right hand came up to massage his thudding forehead, and he stopped again.

"Huh?"

On his close cropped and thinning pate Eric seemed to have sprouted a new head of hair. Not just hair, but a Chia Pet on steroids mane, thick as mink and rakishly long.

"Dream… very weird dream," Eric mumbled, taking note of his new self in the bathroom mirror. He was barefoot but clad in black jeans and a loose white shirt, which even rumpled and slept in looked ridiculously expensive. His face was his own, though now sporting a similarly rakish stubble. And the bone structure itself seemed enhanced — features chiseled and softly hewn, no bags under the eyes. His eyes. The ones staring back at him from the mirror.

As Eric marveled his awareness expanded to note that the bathroom was not done in hastily installed Home Depot veneers and vinyl flooring but black marble, veined with faint spiderlines of silver, azure and rose. The sink was black and glossy, the glass shower next to the Jacuzzi tub massive and sporting enough nozzles to decontaminate radiation victims. It was, plainly put, not Seascape Luxury Apartments, Unit 35.

Eric stepped out of the bathroom cautiously, tanned feet padding across wide-planked hardwood floor. As dreams went it was sure as hell vivid; his senses were settling, further absorbing his strange new surroundings. The roar in his ears receded and clarified into the sound of waves pounding outside the floor to ceiling windows of the bedroom, distanced only by a thin strip of pristine and private beach. The low-slung bed looked vaguely familiar, like the bigger better version of something he had once admired in a Z Gallery showroom. But then so did everything else in the expansive and austere room.

On the floor near the bed was an artful tangle of clothes; some his, then... hers?

Eric reached down and picked up a pair of black lace panties, size two. Then sheer stockings, a black bra, a white blouse and gray skirt, all leading like a trail of breadcrumbs out the bedroom door. A striptease in reverse. As his memory jigsawed into place Eric looked back to the artfully rumpled bed and had erotic flashes of tangled limbs, a tumble of thick dark hair, the smooth moonlit play of skin on skin... and then he realized why he recognized his surroundings.

He should. He wrote them.

Eric was dreaming he was in his movie. Logic stubbornly demanded that much. It was weird but in its own way, kind of cool. Eric turned toward the door, following the trail of castoff clothes, and suddenly stubbed his big toe on the sleek dresser.

"Ow! Shit!" he hissed, grabbing his foot and hopping awkwardly. Dreams weren't supposed to hurt. Suddenly he heard a sound coming from... the kitchen? Yes. He hadn't been there but he saw it in his mind. As he stepped out into the hallway the sound continued; a low slurping sucking gurgle, strange but weirdly familiar.

Eric followed the sound to the end of the hallway. He smelled something. Olfactory trigger. A luscious euphoric recall.

Eric smelled coffee.

The noise was the sound of a coffee maker. Maybe a Braun, definitely German-made. The scent was rich and dark and aromatic. Eric's brain was jellied, thoughts and sensations swirling as he tried to piece them together. A lucid dream, where you know you're dreaming while you're in it? He'd had them before, this was too intense. Psychotic episode? Stress-induced brain fart? Eric didn't know. He just let himself flow with the moment.

Eric stepped around the corner, parsing mental fragments of the woman and the night before...

But the figure that stood on the other side of the kitchen counter was the polar opposite of feminine: hard, swarthy and stocky with pocked skin, black hair pulled back in a braid, muscled arms bulging from a tight white t-shirt. A shoulder rig pinched back his pecs as he poured a steamy mug and slid it across the massive black marble counter.

"Long night, boss?" the hard man said, pouring a cup for himself.

"Uhh…" Eric began, tried again. "Ummm…"

"'Nuff said," The hard man smirked knowingly, and turned to look outside.

Eric picked up the mug, felt it hot in his hands, and took a sip. Dark roast, bitter and bracing. It flooded the crevices of his brain; as it did he took in the whole of the room: huge with a vaulted ceiling and furnished in casual cool, the kitchen area opening up into the greater flow of the space. Grey-green surf crashed outside the windows which comprised the entire side of the house; the sky above it hazy with morning marine layer. The hard man had a tattoo on the back of his neck, four letters inked in Gothic script, two on either side of the braid. T…O… then A…D…

"Toad," Eric mumbled. The hard man turned.

"Yeah boss?" he said.

"What?" Eric said, then remembered. His name is Toad. Of course it was. Eric knew that. He created him, in his mind, and on the page. Nonetheless, his creation was standing there sipping java and staring at him, expecting a reply.

"Nothing…" Eric stammered, then, "Sorry. Brain fried."

"No shit," Toad said. Again with the knowing smirk. "Looks like Trina rode you hard and put you away wet." His voice was gruff with a slight Hispanic lilt, but there was a clear affection there, and even though he looked like he could bend even the buffed Eric into a pretzel he was deferential. Like a wingman. Or a sidekick. Toad nodded to the empty tequila bottle by the sink, the two empty glasses beside it. One of them had a lipstick smear. Eric groaned.

"Giddyup, homes," Toad laughed, then lit a smoke and tossed the pack on the counter. Eric reached for one and fired it up, but as the smoke filled his lungs he suddenly doubled over, coughing and gasping into the sink. He felt like he'd just inhaled sandpaper.

"Geez, Black, since when you smoke?" Toad said, and Eric remembered: Matt Black didn't. Only bad guys did. Something about impressionable kids and role models. Eric looked at the pack: a familiar brand but no product placement. The name said Red Dogs. Matt Black also drank hard liquor, which Eric didn't. Weird.

"Trina," Eric croaked and tossed the smoke. "She around?"

"Do me a favor," Toad said, "don't trust that bitch too much, no matter how good she do you. Use yer big head."

Toad tapped Eric on the forehead and stepped away. As Eric's head cleared he knew: this was not a dream. It was... something else. What exactly, he didn't have a clue. But he knew his script was a hip thriller set in L.A., and here he was, the hip lead. And he knew something else, too: the next words out of Toad's mouth.

"Wakey wakey," Toad said. "Big day today."

Toad tossed Eric a set of keys and Eric caught them instinctively, hand snatching them from mid-air before his brain could even think about it. Toad headed toward the front door, and Eric followed.

As the door opened Eric saw Toad backlit by bright cool light. Just past him in the cloistered driveway sat a midnight blue Acura NSX. Eric's ride. A black Jag was parked beside it: Toad's. Toad paused in the doorway, close enough that Eric could smell his cologne. Toad could smell something, too.

"Meet's at two. Same place," he said, and sniffed. "Hose off the love juice and strap up, bro. Might get a little bumpy."

They said the last line together, in perfect unison. Toad looked at him for a moment, perplexed. Then he climbed into the Jag and pulled out, tires biting the hand laid stones of the drive.

Eric listened as it rounded the corner and zoomed up and out onto the Pacific Coast Highway, heading south to the city. He glanced up: the marine layer was starting to burn off, revealing faint patches of clearest blue.

"Really. Fucking. Weird," Eric said.

He headed back inside, came to the hallway. As he did he heard a hissing sound, saw steam curling from under the bathroom door. Eric approached warily, peeked inside.

The bathroom shower had sprung to life, billows of steam fogging the mirrors and glass, condensing on the marble walls. In the spray he caught glimpse of a beautiful nude woman: her body lithe and tan, long dark wet hair cascading midway down her back. Smallish breasts, sumptuous hips, tiny waist: it struck him, an altogether better, more perfect version of Paige. She cracked open the shower door, smiled slyly. Eric looked at her.

"Trina?"

"He gone?" she asked.

"Toad? Yeah…" he replied.

"What time's the meet?"

"Uhm, two. Same place."

Trina grinned then and pulled him in, hot spray enfolding them as she tugged greedily at his sodden jeans. She kissed his neck, full lips coming up to Eric's ear.

"Don't trust him too much, Black," she whispered. "Use your big head." She nipped his ear, pulling his shirt off. The water was hot, her touch hotter. Eric closed his eyes.

"Uhmmm, what about my little head?" he asked.

"Mmmm. Not so little," she replied, one hand snaking down into his jeans to touch him. She kissed his neck again, as his hands reached around to pull her closer, for a moment lost in what must be the strangest experience of his life. He felt a moment of perfect vertiginous bliss…

…and then his feet slipped, and Eric smacked his head hard on the tile shower walls…

8.

The next thing Eric knew, he was falling: his desk chair tilting back to spill him onto the floor. The chair followed, toppling onto him.

"Ow! Shit!" he croaked, struggling to his feet. The beach house was gone. Trina was gone. His hair was gone. He was back in his little bedroom office, in his real world. Perfect LA morning sun filtered in through the blinds.

"What?" Eric said blearily. Just then his cellphone chirped on his desk: an incoming text. Eric looked at the screen, eyes focusing. Message from Paige: WHERE THE HELL R U??

Eric looked at the digital time display on the LCD screen. 11:45 am.

"Oh no..." he gasped.

It was forty-five minutes later when Eric arrived at HOOYAH!, unshaven and rumpled, his company I.D. hanging from its lanyard around his neck. He had no time to really process the weirdness of what had happened, real life slamming back like a hammer: a placating call to Paige, explaining he couldn't sleep and had walked on the beach — a not unusual occurrence since their move there — then twenty minutes of listening to her cycle through her favorite subject, herself. By the time he rang off, the dream was shredded. Just too much stress meets too overactive an imagination, with an alcohol chaser. Just, weird. But still, it seemed so real...

Eric sat down at his workstation, logged in and slipped on his headset, trying to pretend he'd been there a while. The other workers droned on, oblivious. But a pierced and tatted Goth girl

half his age and three rows over looked up from helping one of
the temps, her big plastic photo I.D. hanging down on her own
lanyard. GILLIAN.

Fuck, Eric thought. Gillian wrapped up with the other temp,
strolled over to Eric.

"Hi," she said, with perfect dotcom corporate casual aplomb.
"Mind if we chat a bit?"

"Sure thing," Eric smiled.

Gillian's office was a corner unit, no window. Floor to ceiling
glass comprised the hall wall, giving the space an airy vibe. Or
like something in a zoo. A desk, a plant, two chairs. Flyers for a
defunct punk band pinned to her personal board. Eric glanced
at them, then away, antsy but subservient, the good worker unit.

Gillian clicked on her keyboard, calling up stats. "Your
numbers are good, Eric — actually you score higher than
anyone in your group." Clickety clickety click. "But you've had
a few lates logging in…"

"Sorry about that," Eric said. "Some stuff came up."

"Problems at home?" Gillian asked.

"No… well, some," Eric offered. "I'm working on a movie
project outside." He swallowed the topsy-turvy taint of outside,
smiled pleasantly. Gillian riffled some papers on her neat desk,
pulled up the print-out of his resumé.

"I saw, you're a writer," she said. "I used to want to write."

"Yeah?" Eric said, deflecting.

"Yeah," Gillian smiled. "I couldn't hack the starving artist
thing. But you…" She read some more. "You're kind of way
over-qualified. If you don't mind me asking, why are you here?"

"Oh, you know," Eric replied. "Just wanted to branch out
into something more… stable…"

Gillian nodded knowingly, put down his file. It was the
perfect business casual conversation: like playing poker. Or
picking flowers in a minefield.

"I get it," she said. "We have a lot of creatives here, Eric. And
you've got a great shot at the next perm slot that opens up. But
we need stability from you, too."

Nice pivot, he thought. Use his own word against him.

Gillian leaned forward like a long lost best friend. "I know you're just a temp now. And we'll work with you on outside interests. But you gotta keep us posted, okay?"

She smiled. He smiled back. Love was in the air.

"You got it," he told her.

9.

The World-Famous Hollywood Magic Castle was a 1909 mansion first built by banker and real estate tycoon Rollin B. Lane, its rich Victorian spires and high peaked roofs overlooking the flat expanse of what now constituted Hollywood. Movies were an embryonic concept at the time; Lane had owned vast swaths of it and dreamt of looking out at orange groves. Drought had other plans. When the Lanes de-camped in the early 1940s they sold off the estate, and the Castle was sub-divided; first into a multi-family home, then a stint as an old folks home, then transformed into a labyrinthine warren of smaller apartments, it glory days far behind it.

In the early 1960s the Castle became a gleam in the eye of one Milt Larsen, a writer on the hit NBC show "Truth or Consequences." Larsen's nine-floor office overlooked the Castle, increasingly overshadowed by the sprawl of LA, and he dreamt of something in honor of his father, a renowned magician. A private club for practitioners of the magical arts.

In 1963 the doors officially opened, and Larsen's dream was made real. A half century-plus later, it still trucked on, tucked up behind Miyagis, where industry hipsters scarfed sushi and sharked their ambition, and largely hidden from street view. It was swanky old school elegance married to close prestidigitation, with private theatres and numerous alcoves tucked into its many twisting staircases. It was a place where up and coming magicians and veterans alike wowed their audiences and kept their skills honed.

Eric sat with Paige and two married friends, midway through the 10 p.m. show in the Castle's *piece de resistance*,

The Palace of Mystery: a former ballroom with a large, velvet curtained stage, and seating for over 100, showcasing stage magic and grand illusion. Entry to the Castle was exclusive — you had to know a member to get on the list — and dress code stifled the tourist trade: cocktail dresses for the women, jacket and tie for men. Paige and her co-worker Linda were stylishly dressed in their corporate upscale best; Eric was paired with Ralph, Linda's husband, mid 50s and laid off, a nice guy and Eric's assumed pal in the marital playdate. Eric was wearing his one good suit. It chafed.

On stage, The Great Whomever was plying his trade: making things appear and disappear with the cunning use of lasers. It was bright and colorful and suitable for Vegas, with fog machines and zippy canned music to highlight the thrills. And though the audience clapped with each new illusion, Eric's mind was utterly elsewhere. In what had happened the other night. In the dream...

Afterwards, Eric and Ralph stood outside, offering the tickets to the valet parking. Eric lit a smoke.

"How's the new job?" Ralph asked.

"Sucks. How's the job hunt?"

"Sucks," Ralph shrugged. He'd been out of work for over forty-seven weeks; mid-management middle-aged white guy, run don't walk to the nearest breadline.

"At least our wives work, huh?"

Just then Paige and Linda came out the front entrance, arm in arm, tipsy, laughing. Paige hugged Linda.

"Thank you so much, we never get out anymore..." she said, and burst out giggling again. Linda caught it too, and the two women leaned into each other. The valet pulled up with Paige's SUV. Eric gave him the ticket and tipped, smiling uneasily.

"What's so funny?" he asked.

"Oh nothing," Paige replied, then busted up again. Frank grinned now, too, wondering what the hell? Finally, Paige explained.

"Some woman in the bathroom was complaining about finding her prince on a white horse..." she began. Linda chimed in.

"...and Paige said, 'I found mine, but he was riding a donkey!'"

The two women laughed again, lost in hilarity. Eric and Frank looked at each other like, and the funny part is?

The ride home was silent: Eric driving, Paige picking up on the absence of small talk.

"That was fun," she said.

"Yeah," Eric answered. "Fun."

She looked at him. "God, what's your problem?" she asked, perplexed and annoyed.

Eric drew a breath, weighing his words. "You remember when you first came here, how you said you never wanted to be an "LA Woman"?" he explained. "Congrats, hon. You just became one."

Paige went defensive. "Frank's been looking for work, too. It was just a joke."

"At my expense?"

"I tried to do something nice for you. Get you out of your funk."

"I'm not in 'a funk'," Eric said. "I'm just stressed."

"Well, how do you think I feel?"

Eric said nothing, just drove. Paige stared out the passenger window sullenly.

"You're an ass," she muttered.

10.

Home. Late. Eric sat in his office, his laptop in front of him. Wondering. But just as he touched fingers to keyboard, something shifted in his peripheral vision: Paige, in the doorway, in a nightgown, long dark hair loose, still tipsy, but with an attitude. She saw the way he looked at her and bristled.

"What?" she asked.

"Nothing," Eric said. "What's up?"

She crossed her arms. "Are you ever going to fuck me again?"

Nice. Eric muttered, "Maybe I don't fuck people who make me feel bad about myself..."

"What?" she said, not hearing.

"Nothing," Eric sighed.

They lay in the darkened back bedroom, on the wrought iron bed: a man and woman, naked, engaged in what might at best be considered the dullest missionary coitus on record. For Eric, all sense of passion and heat and hunger had been extinguished — ebbing for perhaps years before, but most certainly guttered with her recent revelation of him ruining her life.

As such, whatever might have been their innate chemistry — its nascent romanticism worn down by marriage and alienation — had simply flatlined in him. There was no connection, no sense of heat and frission, no joining together on any level. As for her, he knew not what might have been going on inside — she exhibited no tactile woman sense, and her beauty to him was rendered merely doll-like. He was, plainly put, servicing her, at the altar of her own highly attuned sense of self-worth.

This was Jiffy Lube sex, perfunctory and about as exciting as an erotic oil change.

Worse yet when she'd had a few drinks; her libido was larger by far than her skill set, and sloppy didn't add to the festivities. Eric had had great lovers before; Paige was the first who could actually make a blowjob boring. It wasn't a lack of inhibition. It was, simply, a lack of skill.

They switched and he went down — a paint-by-numbers adventure, like the late Sam Kinison's joke about licking the alphabet. Paige moaned quietly from some distant inner place — no build to a carnal crescendo, no rising tide of woman lust carrying him over the edge at that critical moment. Just, moan... moan... moan... gasp.

Then she came, short and sharp. A man-gasm. His marital duty was done. But then...

"What about you?" her voice, small and out of breath. Eric knew the drill: he switched and got into position.

And it was here that Eric deployed a small secret: dangerous and heretical. As he went through the motions he flashed on its origins; roughly two years before, when in the midst of their ongoing disenfranchisement she had uttered that one potent unto withering four-letter word. BABY.

She hadn't said it with any perceivable heart; what's more, Eric could not recall her ever expressing any innate maternal sense whatsoever — with other women's children, or in general. She did not smile at children on the street; he did. She did not play with other people's kids; he did. It was just something to be done for her, on the way to other things to be done. It seemed totemic — a life marker to hit on her dream train, which his own unraveling had inadvertently de-railed.

It was at the subsequent moment she had informed him she was going to stop taking birth control that he had gone to the other extreme: he had simply stopped fucking her, or at least winnowed it down to barest maintenance sex. Easy enough to do, when every other word out of her mouth was a scalding critique on his failure. Easy enough to fake, when she didn't seem to notice.

Eric grunted and thrust and played his part, fairly secure

that she either did not know or would not care. He'd written enough hot love scenes and had a few in real life for reference; he could phone this part in.

Eric played off his big finish and rolled away, staring at the ceiling. The overhead fan twirled lazily, mute witness. Guess men can fake orgasms, too, he thought, as Paige curled over, her back to him, and slipped off to boozy sleep.

He watched the fan for another twenty minutes, listening to her breathing. Thinking about Trina, and the very odd dream.

And of going there again.

11.

Depression. A black hole sucking at the pit of his soul, like a stinking drain, dragging in all strength, all hope, all light. Leaving in its wake only a residue of ceaseless despair. Stomach tightened into a double fist, pushing up his larynx. Chest constricted, breath coming in short, hyperventilating gasps he could scarcely control. Thoughts churning like a whirlpool. Every mistake he ever made. Every right that ever turned wrong. Every dream ever dashed on the rocks. All replayed over and over and over, with this singular self-referencing mantra as a soundtrack:

I hate you I hate you I hate you I hate you…

Past in ashes. Future terrifying. Present, unrelenting and bad. Nowhere, safe. Nothing, good. Feeble awareness that, yes, life is beautiful. Just not his. All beauty and hope and caring, something reserved for others more deserving. As if life itself had downsized, and he didn't even rate the memo to clean out his desk.

It came like a stagnant tide: rolling in, but not retreating. It could go on for hours, days, weeks, months. Sometimes just a sour hollow feeling permeating everything, often so crushing it blotted out anything in its path. Until it took hours to muster every ounce of the strength he no longer possessed, just to get up and take a piss.

Eric rose on unsteady legs and made his way out of the bedroom. His attacks annoyed Paige, who, when privy, said she needed her sleep… she had to work, make money, support them. Sticking it in deeper, and twisting.

He fumbled down the hall in jeans and t-shirt, barefoot, eyes closed, breath rasping, trying to not make noise. He felt along the walls to the living room, found the reclining chair, climbed in, tilted back. He wished he could just blow a hose — heart attack, aneurysm, stroke — just die, cash out, cease to be. Better for him, better for everyone. Part of him marveled at the dumb tenacity of the machine that was his flesh. Heart still beating, blood still flowing. Brain, still thinking. But of nothing good.

He closed his eyes against the streetlights outside. Outer stimuli hurt — sound, sight, smell, touch. Inside stimuli — thought, feeling, memory — hurt worse. He was trapped in his own skin, his own mind and soul. He craved blackness and oblivion — to not think, not be. His legs trembled and shook in ragged polyrhythms, which left unchecked, would radiate up to encompass his entire body, like a seizure of the mind rendered physical and relentless.

He felt stupid, pathetic, useless, weak. He had no one to blame but himself, and sought no forgiveness. Doing the best he could didn't count, not in the real world. Success was the only measure. Failure was not an option. Everything else was for the mass grave — of a brutal, stupid culture; a brutal, stupid economy; a brutal, stupid century. In which he no longer felt a place worth being.

When will you admit it's over for you? Her words stinging him like rock salt rubbed into flayed flesh. He tried to imagine other Erics he should be, could not. Not after one thousand unanswered résumés underscored his lack of worth. Not after the one came back, offering him temporary peonage.

Spiritual palliatives — seek his inner self, connect with his greater power — met only silence. God was a busy guy, and Eric's guardian angels weren't returning his calls. Everything happened for a reason, but the reason for this seemed simply, stress test to fail point. Not dead yet. Pile a little more on. Like the snarky "de-motivational" poster he once saw, a send-up of corporate rah-rah art: the bow of a ship slipping beneath polar waters, and the legend: Maybe The Purpose Of Your Life Is To Serve As a Warning To Others...

Eric gasped, teeth chattering now. Control this, he thought. Stop... stop... stop....

There was a noise outside the window. Eric cracked his slit eyes open: through the picture window he saw the pretty neighbor, coming home. She was dressed in sheer white pants cut up to mid thigh, knee high black boots, a light leather blazer over a low cut top. She was lovely. She was not alone.

Good for her, Eric thought, and closed his eyes again. Good for her.

He slid back into his private hell. Until sheer exhaustion finally claimed him.

12.

The rest of the weekend passed without incident; no strange dreams, no more panic attacks, no odd and inexplicable disappearances. But also, no writing: Eric had gnawed at the edges of the latest draft, making cosmetic changes. Perhaps waiting for today, and the meeting, but also with a sense of trepidation: a gut reluctance to dive back in. The down time had been spent in predictably domesticity: go to the gym with Paige, go grocery shopping with Paige, watch a DVD with Paige. Clean the apartment, without Paige. Some divisions remained clear.

As he made his way through the Warner Brothers lot and down the winding garden path to the bungalows he thought about the last line on his screen when he opened the draft back up again. It said, plainly:

```
...and then his feet slipped, and Matt Black
smacked his head hard on the tile shower walls...
```

...which was not in the script, nor was it supposed to be in the script, nor in any scene he had ever consciously written. Key word, consciously, he amended. Who the fuck knows what I wrote half passed out? He had deleted and corrected, then emailed the draft over to Marty's office, and tried to put it out of his mind.

But it would not go. Whatever had happened, it not only felt as real as life, it felt better than life. For a fleeting elastic moment of subconscious sensory overload, he had felt... good, for the first time in a long time. Like he had accidentally tripped into an altogether better world, which existed only in his mind. And on paper, in the printout of his overactive imagination.

It frightened him. It excited him. And strangely, he wanted more.

But first things first.

13.

The heart of Martin Blumenthal Productions were nested in a series of second floor offices, their exterior all stucco and red tile roofing, sleekly reeking of old Hollywood. Rumor had it that Dean Martin had personally puked in Marty's bathroom, back in the Rat Pack days.

Eric sat in an austere conference room, all glass and black marble. Awards and plaques adorned shelves on one wall, tributes to the magic Blumenthal touch. Emmys and lesser achievements, but no Oscar, its absence conspicuously evident by a space reserved for it. Which, Eric noted privately, he was unlikely to get anytime soon, given his tastes in projects, Eric's own offering inclusive. TURNAROUND had begun with noble enough intentions, and a solid enough script. But along the way were added the dreaded notes and changes — a heist, a double cross, the ubiquitous love triangle, ad nauseum — until it reached the point where even Eric wasn't sure what the movie was about anymore, he just wanted to get it made. But God help him if he ever admitted that.

His cell phone vibrated. He glanced down, saw the name. PAIGE. He let it go to voicemail.

"Mr. Best," Marty said pleasantly, strolling in with his assistant Todd in tow. "How's it hangin'?"

Marty was in his fifties, tall and thin and oozing casual success; artfully greyed hair combed back, button-down shirt untucked over crisp jeans, no socks, an aging ex-surfer trust fund baby with a three thousand dollar watch. Todd was mid-twenties, slight, an aspiring actor new to the town and the biz, and smart enough to keep his mouth shut. He took a seat at the table with pen and legal pad, ready to catch the brilliance as it flew.

"Hangin' heavy, Mister B.," Eric replied. "How was Japan?"

"Exhausting, exciting," Marty chimed. "Ever been to Tokyo? Nothing like it. You gotta go."

Eric nodded — of course he gotta. It was the kind of pitch perfect facile tone that the town loved — project abject confidence at all times. Success was magnetic; failure was regarded as a virulent and possibly contagious from of cancer. He pulled his own pen and notebook, readying himself. Across the room a big dry-wipe board graced the wall: TURNAROUND was written there, along with the titles of a half dozen other shots at celluloid glory. On the far side of the glass conference room wall, movie posters flanked the outer office. Thrillers, straight to DVD horror, movies with numbers in the titles, a few impressive indies, an HBO miniseries. Some Eric had seen and liked — he knew Marty was capable of good work; others he had literally felt the brain cells dying as he tried to watch them. But they all got made.

"So," Marty began. "The new draft…"

Eric clicked his pen, ready to deface his latest efforts. Todd watched dutifully, his own pen poised for backup.

"The new draft," Eric echoed. "You like?"

"I love," Marty answered, continuing his stroll, fingers steepled to signal deep thinkee mode. If experience was any judge, this was where he'd start offering adjectives like puzzle pieces for Eric to decode. Like reading tea leaves. Or goat entrails. "But it still needs… I don't know… brio?"

"Brio?" Eric asked.

"Vervacity, verve…" Todd offered, helpful. Eric took the effort and tried to narrow Marty's concern.

"It's not lively enough?"

"It is," Marty said. "But… Black is still kind of dark…"

Eric scribbled notes, ventured a defense. "He's Matt Black," he said. "It's a dark thriller…"

Marty picked up on the reticence. "Don't get me wrong, Eric. I love dark. It's edgy. It's what this script needs and it's got it in spades. But it still needs…"

"More light?" Eric offered.

"Exactly," Marty smiled. "Some light to pierce Black's darkness. Maybe humor. Not funny ha-ha, just…"

"Irony?" Eric said.

"Yes." Marty brightened. "I mean, Black's a great character, he's got his world by the balls…"

"But everyone is trying to kill him and he doesn't know who to trust…"

"Yes, and that's great," Marty said. "But he should be ironic about it." He paused, leaned in for effect. "You know, Cage might be interested in playing him…"

Eric was surprised. "Can we afford him?"

"If he says yes, we can," Marty answered assuredly. "His last movie did a hundred and eighty mil. But he's looking to break out of his rut… he wants to stretch. If we can give Black some irony, maybe laced with pathos…"

"But with brio, less dark, no jokes…" Eric scribbled.

"Exactly," Marty beamed. "We're counting on you, Eric. We're close on this one. Real close. One more tweak and…"

Marty let it dangle. Eric scribbled some more and nodded.

"You got it," he said.

In the California Wellness Center, Gabe looked at Eric, quietly sizing him up. Eric sat, uncharacteristically silent. His coffee sat, untouched. Major red flag.

"How are you feeling? Gabe ventured.

"Like a man who's writing for his life," Eric said. Gabe smiled ruefully, nodded.

"Don't get me wrong," Eric continued. "I respect Marty, he's done a lot of movies. But it's like these guys can only think of what the last big box office is or who the next big star is. No sooner than I finish one draft he wants me to chase the last hit. It's like driving down a road you've never been down before with the windshield painted black, navigating by what you see in the rearview mirror. You can never catch up. I fucking hate it."

"Why don't you quit?" Gabe asked.

"And do what?" Eric shot back. "Besides, writing is the only place I can go to that still feels good. Fucked as this is, my movie feels more real than my life."

Gabe thought about that a moment, intrigued. "I love the metaphor," he said. "We're all living in our own movie, you know. Everyone's the hero of their own drama…"

"Some heroes are better than others." Eric took a sip of the now lukewarm coffee. "Ever hear of lucid dreaming?

"Of course," Gabe answered. "You're dreaming but you're aware…"

"…and you can alter the flow of the dream without waking up," Eric continued, "Yeah. I'd done it before, even when I didn't know what it was called." He paused, then said, "but now it's like it's bleeding into my work."

"How so?" Gabe scribbled something on his notepad.

"I was working the other night…" Eric sighed. "Paige and I had another fight. I fell asleep writing, and I had this dream. I thought I was awake at first, but… I dunno." He stopped, pondering. "It was so real…"

"Were you in control of it? The dream, I mean…"

"Yes," Eric said, then, "sort of. But then… not. Like the dream was dreaming me while I was dreaming it." Eric shrugged and made a booga booga sound. Oooh, spooky.

Gabe smiled, scribbled something else. "Maybe your subconscious is trying to tell you something?" he offered.

That I've finally lost my mind?" Eric laughed, then, "Thing is, it was weird, but I liked it," he said.

"You liked it…" Gabe repeated. "Why?"

"I was a better 'me'," Eric confessed. "And I felt some control over things."

Gabe nodded and scribbled. Eric sighed.

"I didn't want to leave."

14.

Eric arrived home late, hustled across the Seascape courtyard and took the steps two at a time, heading for his apartment. Paige would be home soon; he had to get dinner made. As he reached the top step the door to Unit 34 opened directly before him and the neighbor stepped out, almost running into him. She smiled, flustered.

"Oh, hi!" she said.

"Sorry!" Eric blurted.

"You must be the new neighbor," she said. "I'm Kate."

"Eric, hi…" he smiled.

Just then a big lummox of a man stepped out from the doorway behind her. He was tall and porcine, with gimlet eyes and a tidy black moustache, utterly humorless. "Um, Eric, this is my friend Stewart…" she said.

"Hi," Eric said. Stewart nodded in response, and his hand slipped around Kate's waist. The gesture said more than friends; it said mine.

"We better go," he told her.

Eric stepped aside to let them pass. Kate smiled again, something vaguely unsettling behind it.

"Nice meeting you," she said.

"You too," Eric replied. As they went down the stairs it occurred to him they looked weird together, an odd fit, but whatever. Eric glanced at his watch.

"Shit," he muttered.

Eric was busily stir-frying when Paige arrived. The usual routine. Drop the attaché. Hang up the scarf. Charge the

Blackberry. Law & Order on the tube. Glass of wine poured. But when he went to give her the perfunctory kiss, she turned her head.

"You don't answer my calls now?" she said.

"I had my cell off," he said. "I was in the meeting with Marty. He wants another draft."

"Uh-huh," she snorted derisively. "When's he going to pay you?"

Eric put a plate of food in front of her. "Not soon enough," he sighed.

"That's just great," Paige muttered, stabbing stir-fry with her fork. "I knew this was going to happen." She picked up her plate and moved over to the sofa. Eric poured himself a glass of wine and started toward the hall, thinking, of course you did.

"You're not going to eat?" she asked.

"Not hungry," he replied. And left her to it.

Eric's office was dark and quiet. Door, closed; windows, open. A gentle sea breeze wafted through. It was hours later, and Paige had long since gone to bed, their evening's fight rendered merely an installment. He sat at his desk, drumming his fingers expectantly, staring at the laptop screen. Totally brain-locked. He popped one of Gabe's meds, chased it down with wine. Then reached into his pocket, pulled out his flash drive, plugged it in to an empty port. The little blue LED on it glowed dutifully.

On the laptop screen, the words CUT TO sat there, insert point blinking expectantly. Taunting him.

Eric sighed and leaned in; suddenly, there was a commotion outside. He tilted back in his chair, peered through the window.

Kate and Stewart were at her front door, back from their night out. She was clearly two sheets to the wind, and pissed. Stewart stood behind her as she fumbled with the lock: a hulking presence. He muttered something. Kate's head whipped around.

"Will you shut up?" she said. "God I fucking hate you…"

The door opened then and she entered, tried to slam it on him. But Stewart caught it and let himself in, closing it behind them. The muffled sounds of argument continued inside.

Eric leaned back, but not before catching another glimpse:

of Marin, seated on her stoopside perch, quaffing box wine and smoking. Her back was to the drama but Eric could feel her, drinking it all in.

"Gawd," he muttered. "No joy in Mudville tonight..."

Eric turned back to the laptop, and the task at hand. He tapped at the keys, muttering more.

"Irony... pathos...brio... too dark... more light... dark "lite"..." He tapped some more. "Bullshit, bullshit, bullshit, bullshit..."

He hit the delete key, dumping entire scenes, pages scrolling backwards into digital oblivion, feeling some grim satisfaction at watching them disappear. He let up and the insert cursor held, blinking. Like a dare. Or an invitation.

"Fuck it," Eric sighed. And started to write.

And as he released himself into it — forgetting about drama and stress and pressure and failure, jettisoning all the bent fucked relationships and everything but the now of this moment — his fingers moved faster, words and images spilling out of his mind and onto the screen. Eric stared intently, his fingers moving faster... and faster... the power of word and thought incarnate sucking him in...

15.

...and then Eric was whipping the NSX south on the Pacific Coast Highway, knifing through traffic, windows open, the wind in his hair. The car was sleek and fast and responsive; his grip on the leather-clad wheel firm and assured. The vista before him was spectacular: the sweep of PCH as it serpentined through the passes, high mansioned-topped hills to one side, the broad glittering arc of the Pacific to the other. The colors were vivid yet subtly over-saturated, like a Maxfield Parish painting on Ecstasy; he could smell the brine on the sea air. It was a world of his own imagining yet infused with a life all its own; Eric felt a tingling sensation on the small hairs of his arms and neck, as if this world knew him but studied him on a cellular level. He punched the gas, the speedometer arcing up to sixty, seventy, eighty. He didn't worry about cops. He hadn't written any into this scene. He felt alive. He felt calm and in control...

...until he reached the last leg, where PCH flattened out beneath the Santa Monica bluffs, and traffic stopped dead. Gridlock. Eric looked around: on the wide flat beach tanned and buff young people were playing volleyball; surfers were tagging the crests of waves; a pelican did a dive-bomb for aquatic din-din. Eric glanced at his three thousand dollar watch: 1:45 pm. He'd be late for the meet.

"Fuck it," Eric said, then punched it and lurched out of his lane, crossing the median and heading straight into northbound traffic, dodging honking cars and trucks like two-ton Tonkas. His timing was razored-edge perfect, barely missing a dozen times, only to pick up even more speed. The NSX purred, begging for more. Eric was about to oblige...

...when he suddenly caught glimpse of a lemon-yellow Hummer fishtailing and careening into his path. A T-boned broadside was imminent, inescapable...

...and Eric said, "STOP!"

And then everything did — Eric's car, the Hummer, all of the other traffic. There was no neck-snapping crunch, just a weird flutter in the pit of his stomach. Whoa, he thought, and looked around.

Across the beach — indeed, across the entire landscape — everything had halted as if frozen in time. On the beach volleyball game, a pretty Asian girl in a bikini hung airborne in mid-spike, her hair splayed in the breeze which had ceased to flow. The surfers crested still-life waves like glistening statues. The pelican was caught in mid-splash, its webbed feet sticking up from the plume.

The NSX's engine was still running, a low smooth idle. Eric touched the gas and gently eased himself around the frozen pileup in progress. As he drove back over the median into his own lane and stopped, looked back. Thought about it a moment.

"Go," he said quietly.

Instantly, life resumed. The girl made the spike. The pelican got its meal. The surfers rode their waves. Even the Hummer re-gained control and swerved back into lane, honking its horn as it roared away.

"Cool," Eric muttered, running his hand through his hair. Just then the car behind him nudged up, honking impatiently. Eric looked ahead: his lane was open. He stuck his left hand out the window, waved bye-bye to the pissed-off driver.

Then sped his cool car and bad self off.

16.

The meet was in a parking structure: upper level, low lit, desolate. Eric wheeled the car into an empty slot, got out, carrying a brushed metal attaché case. He checked his watch. 1:55.

Something moved in the periphery — Eric looked up and saw Toad and Trina step out from the shadows at different angles. Like Eric, they were both dressed in black; Trina wore a leather trench coat, tight black catsuit, and knee high black boots, her dark hair pulled back; Toad carried an AR-15 with a silencer and laser sight on it. They triangulated as Eric approached.

"You know what to do," he said, because that's what he was supposed to say. He was living the play-pretend of the scripted moment and digging it. "Anyone in Tio's crew so much as twitches, you drop 'em."

"You got it," Toad replied. He smiled like he hoped they would, then headed off to take a backup position. As Eric turned Trina suddenly took his hand.

"Black, I'm nervous," she said. Her eyes radiated taut, catlike wariness.

"Don't be," Eric told her. "Just do your job."

He started to let go. She was still holding on. She suddenly pulled him close, and he could feel the heat of her. She nailed him with a hot, lingering kiss. Eric enfolded her in a steamy embrace, ran one hand through her thick blonde hair, then…

"Wait, what?" he said, confused. "Stop!"

He pulled back. Trina was frozen in place like a living mannequin — eyes closed, red lips parted, head tilted in a forever kiss. But she was wearing sheer white pants cut to mid-thigh, a light leather blazer over a low cut top, knee high boots.

Legs that went on forever. She did not look like an idealized version of Paige anymore. She looked like his neighbor, Kate.

Eric stepped away — pulse pounding, whole body breaking into a light-sheened sweat. His temples thudded. Eric felt a lurching rush of vertigo and doubled over, hands coming up to grip his skull...

... and then he was back in his office, back in the real world. He sat up in his chair, breath heaving as the feelings receded. His vision swam, blurred for an instant, then fixated on the glowing laptop screen. Eric shook it off and read his last words typed there:

```
TIGHT ON ERIC as he enfolds Trina in a steamy
embrace. He runs one hand through her thick
blonde hair...
```

He hit delete, changed blonde to dark. Sat back. Glanced over through the window, at Kate's apartment. The lights were off. Quiet now. In for the night.

"Jesus," he muttered. He felt oddly drained.

He copied the script onto the little flash drive, pulled it from the slot, held it up. The little blue LED stayed on a moment, then winked off.

Weird, he thought.

17.

The next day, Eric sat at his workstation, bored to utter numbness. The sound from his headset leaked out, tinny in the air. A coquettish young woman in a Japanese schoolgirl's outfit was bouncing on the screen, straddling a Sybian — a black naugahyde-covered hemispheric cylinder with a little motor inside and controls that looked like they were pieced together from Frankenstein's lab, with a pallid nubbed latex dildo stuck in the middle of it, and rubbing up against her. The woman cooed.

"Ooooh do me daddy… I'm a bad little girl…"

The Sybian made a noise like a leaf blower. An unseen man's hands loomed into frame and cranked the voltage. The young woman moaned in what was very likely quite authentic orgasmic abandon. Eric approved and denied the last of submitted terms and clicked off. He looked at his tally for the day — seventeen hundred and eighty. He'd been at it all day. His head wanted to explode.

Eric looked around. No one was paying any attention. He reached into his pocket, pulled out the flash drive. Plugged it into a port on the workstation.

Eric started to write.

Gillian was making her rounds, tending her crew, overseeing production, when she glanced over and saw Eric at his station, four rows over. Just then Jennifer came up.

"Gill, do we still have the staff meeting?" she asked.

"Yeah," Gillian replied. "Ten minutes."

"Right, thanks." Jennifer hustled off.

Gillian smiled and glanced back. Something was off. It took her a moment to realize that Eric was gone. She looked across the expanse of the floor: no Eric, anywhere. And no way he could have crossed the room that fast.

Gillian walked over to his station, saw a blank screen, but still logged in. She glanced down and saw the little flash drive poking out of the slot, LED softly pulsing. She thought about pulling it, thought again.

Gillian frowned.

18.

Kid Rock pounded from the penthouse suite: the city lights glittered from a world class view. A hydroponically beautiful bim with very long legs and a very short skirt popped the cork on a bottle of Dom, bubbles pluming. Toad threw fistfuls of cash in the air, hundreds fluttering down around them as he grabbed the bim by the waist.

The bim giggled. Just then Eric entered, clad entirely in black. Toad looked at him and beamed.

"Who da man?" He said. "Who da motherfuckin' man!!"

He released the bim and grabbed Eric in a meaty man hug, hoisting him in the air. Eric looked beat but relieved, alert. He patted Toad on the back warmly.

"Way to go, bro," he said. "You did good." He looked around. "Where's Trina?"

"I'm here, baby…" Eric turned and saw Trina standing in the bedroom doorway, wearing nothing but one of his impossibly expensive shirts. Eric went to her, wrapped his arms around her and picked her up, spinning her as she ran her hands through his hair.

"You were amazing," he said.

"So were you," she replied, then whispered, "I got you a present."

Eric put her down. She smiled slyly and led him by his Italian silk tie into the master bedroom: massive, opulent. On the king-sized bed Eric saw another woman leaning back on a sea of crisp hundred dollar bills, wearing Trina's trenchcoat, black thigh-highs, and nothing else. She looked from Eric to Trina and smiled.

"Starting the party without me?" he said.

"Mmmm," Trina cooed. "You are the party."

She pushed him down onto the bed, ripping open his shirt and kissing his neck. The other woman moved in from the other side, nibbling and nipping at his throat. They kissed him, then each other. Eric's eyes fluttered back; his entire body went flush with sweat. He felt one brief, deliriously ecstatic moment...

...followed by a stabbing pain as if someone had plunged a screwdriver between his eyes...

...and the next thing Eric knew he was back in his Aeron chair, at his workstation: head tilted back, a thin arc of drool leaking from the corner of his mouth. He sat upright, completely disoriented, then looked around.

Night had fallen outside. The vast room's lights had dimmed to Twilight mode. A handful of third shift drones huddled at their distant workstations, staring at their screens, oblivious. Eric looked at his watch. 8:40.

I am so fucked, he thought.

19.

The beach was deserted. The night tide rolled in and out, waves rippling onto the sand then sucking back out with a soft hissing sound. Eric walked at water's edge; shoes off, pants rolled up, surf sloshing up to his knees. It was oddly calming in a world that was anything but. At least, not his own.

He gazed across the broad expanse of beach to the lights on Esplanade, the many homes and apartments and condos and abodes, and thought, whatever hells the residents there suffered, they did it with one hell of a view.

He had not gone home yet. If experience were any judge he could only imagine what awaited. Weirder still, he had not gotten a single call or text from Paige. Which, though merciful in the interim, only meant worse coming when he finally stepped through the door.

He didn't care anymore — the marriage could not be more dead if it stepped out of a zombie movie and tried to eat his brain. It was simply a matter of how much more before done was done.

And he had other problems.

His sanity, for one. In real time he had been gone for almost five hours, from when he had first plugged the flash drive in. There was no direct connect between time in the real world and Time in what he had come to think of as scriptworld. It seemed to run on its own clock: subservient to him to a point, but with a pulse all its own.

There was no way for him to explain what had happened to him, either. It was apparent enough, having written and tripped into his scriptworld, he simply did not exist in this one.

The operative word being, tripped. Eric had no idea whatsoever how he entered scriptworld — like a man with a door for which he had many keys, but a different one worked at any time. It seemed to hinge on focus and surrender, in the Zen sense — when he simply let go in the writing, it sucked him in to wherever he was in the story. And he was the only one who knew.

Exit was another issue entirely. Not only could he but barely control entry, staying there was an altogether different issue. Staying took a toll, took energy, tapped him. He could feel the draining each time he entered, wondered what indeed it was using up.

But stay, he wanted. Badly.

Like the scene he'd just written. It was juvenile and over the top, and back in the penthouse location Marty had instructed him to cut. But he'd written it for the hell of it, written it for himself, just to see what it felt like. It didn't matter that he'd change it later; it existed in the moment, and the moment was fine. And so long as he controlled it, no one was the wiser.

Eric felt a rush of guilty pleasure, dampened by the knowledge that he in fact did not control this newfound power. But he needed to. He'd fed so much of his life into writing this thing that it had come to life.

And increasingly, it felt like the only life worth having.

Eric looked out at the sea, the dark horizon there. It was almost 10 pm. The horizon offered no answers. He didn't expect any.

He'd have to find them for himself.

20.

The apartment was quiet when he entered; the light on the dining room table, on. A wine bottle and glass, empty. Dinner plate, left out. Ashtray, bristling with cigarette butts. Blackberry, charging on table. A still life, painted in estrangement.

Eric moved down the darkened hallway. The bedroom door was closed, a faint sliver of light peeking out. He thought about entering, did not. As he turned to his office, it winked out.

Eric sat at his desk. He'd been trying to write for the last hour, steeped in oppressive silence, marred only by the noise in his head. His thoughts kept turning to the closed doors, the yawning chasm between them. He existed only as a symbol for her frustration, a ceremonial dumping ground for all bad in her world. He could no longer feel any love from her, nor any for her at all.

The windows were open. The courtyard itself was eerily quiet: even Marin was not on her stoop. He heard soft breeze riffling the palm trees, the low tinkling of the little fountain near the pool. The script document was open on his laptop. But he could not find his way in, could not lose himself. Eric leaned in, trying to concentrate.

Suddenly there was a noise — muffled, angry words, behind closed doors. A flash of frenetic, kinetic motion. Eric glanced outside, saw the door to Unit 34 open: Kate stood, backlit, angry.

"Bastard!" she said. The door closed, hard.

Silence. Doesn't sound good, Eric thought, then turned his attention back to the script, and Matt Black. Matt Black was confident. Eric was not. Matt Black was strong. Eris was not.

Matt Black was cool. Eric was a train wreck...
...so just project the opposite of me and I've nailed him, Eric
thought. He started to write. Tappity tappity tap.
Then outside, more noise. Kate's front door opened. More
angry words. Harsher this time. Heated.
"No! Get AWAY from me!"
The door slammed shut. Eric sighed. Whatever was
happening there was bad. Whatever was happening there was
none of his business. He tried to concentrate... Matt Black, Matt
Black, thriller, thriller, cool, cool, irony, irony...
... tappity tappity....
Her door opened again. Violent now.
"NO! I want you OUT of here!"
A muffled reply. Kate slammed the door again.
"What the fuck..." Eric sighed.

He stood at the door to Unit 34, feeling like a total idiot. He
knew he should mind his own business. He should go back
to his solitary hell. He should call the cops and stay out of it.
But there was a vibe in the air — deeper than cheap drama,
something toxic and dangerous. Like something very bad was
about to happen, and he was the only one who might be able to
head it off.
He reached up to knock. But just as he did the door opened
again, and Kate was there — disheveled, distraught. Their eyes
met, mutual surprise.
"Hi," he said. "Are you okay?"
Kate started to cry and walked back to her kitchen counter,
leaving the door hanging open, Eric standing at the threshold.
She poured some wine from a bottle on the counter.
Eric wavered, then stepped inside, closing the door but
leaving it ajar. Kate's brow furrowed as she fought back the
tears, one hand coming up to her temple. She shook her head.
"I'm sorry," she said. "I want him out. He won't leave."
She gestured past Eric to Stewart, who sat lumpenly on
Kate's IKEA sofa, staring at the TV in quiet truculence. The
apartment itself was a chaotic shithole: castoff clothes and
detritus sprawled everywhere, evidence not of a fight but a life

gone desperately off the rails. It seemed a stark contradiction to her sunny outward persona. Stewart's bag was packed and by the sofa. Eric looked at it, then at Stewart, who would not meet his gaze.

"Crazy bitch…" he muttered sullenly.

Kate snapped then, lunging at him in alcohol-fueled anger. Eric caught her, trying to keep her back. But instead of fighting him she went fragile, quivering with frustrated and inchoate rage.

"I want him out I want him out he's a fucking liar…" she murmured.

Eric felt like a man who'd stepped into a puddle and sank over his head: sudden referee to a domestic disturbance on the brink. Something in him hardened; he ignored Stewart and comforted Kate.

"Everything's okay," he told her. "Just calm down…"

But Kate just pulled away and stalked into the hallway, slamming the bedroom door. Behind him Stewart got up off the sofa, starting to follow. Eric's arm shot out, finger pointing into the bigger man's face.

"Stay…" he said.

Stewart stayed.

Eric knocked softly on the bedroom door, waited, heard soft sobbing. He entered cautiously: the room was dark, light from the windows rendering her in stark and poignant shadow. Around her, more chaos, more clutter. Kate sat on the rumpled bed, head in her hands, fingers twined through blonde hair.

There was no place to sit. Eric knelt gingerly by the end of the bed.

"It's all my fault," she said haltingly. "I invited him here. But I want him to go now and he won't…"

She stifled another sob, tried to compose herself. "He just won't go…" she repeated, despairing.

"Okay," Eric said softly. "It's gonna be okay. You stay here, all right?"

She nodded, not looking up. Eric exited the bedroom, quietly closed the door behind him.

Back in the living room, Stewart was back on the sofa, staring at the muted TV. Something about him rankled Eric to the bone: beyond his piggish glare and innate obstinance, his obvious insensitivity and obnoxious entitlement. His whole vibe radiated: this guy is enjoying this. He likes making her cry. Something clicked in Eric's psyche: beyond loathing, just flat resolve.

"She wants you gone," Eric told him.

Stewart looked up at Eric, hostile and defensive. "No way, man," he blurted, "I live in Idaho, she invited me out here, my plane doesn't leave for two days."

"You got nowhere to go tonight?" Eric asked. "Come back tomorrow, try to sort it out?"

The second he said it Eric knew he'd made a mistake. The very question offered an implied negotiation. Stewart instinctively seized the moment, standing up.

"Fuck that. I ain't leavin'," Stewart said. He called out past Eric.

"Yo, KATE!!"

Stewart got up from the sofa started to walk past Eric, all hard fat and attitude. Eric stepped in front of him, his right hand planting on Stewart's sternum, fingers stiff and jutting.

"No," Eric said.

And that was when things moved almost freakishly quickly. Kate's erstwhile suitor and four inches and forty pounds on Eric, but Eric could smell the booze on his breath. And there was something else — something indefinable uncoiling in Eric's soul, a feeling he had not felt in a long, long time. Quiet, certain, primal strength.

Eric pushed him back a step and Stewart went Raging Bull, throwing a big sloppy roundhouse at Eric's head. Eric pivoted back, Stewart's meaty hand missing him by an inch. But instead of backing up, Eric stepped in: body blocking the bigger man as Eric elbowed him in the solar plexus. Stewart whuffed as the air leaked out of him and Eric grabbed him by the shirt collar, placing one foot behind Stewart and giving a small but forceful push. Stewart tilted back, off balance, and Eric pressed forward, gripping his shirt, letting gravity do the rest.

Stewart dropped, Eric's weight coming down onto him, one knee landing hard on the lummox's stomach as the other planted square in the crux of his left armpit, pinning the arm as it short-circuited the nerve nexus there.

It was over in four seconds. Stewart's eyes swam in his thick face; in the heat of the moment the subtlety was lost that the only person perhaps more surprised than Stewart, was Eric. He leaned in, grimly hissing.

"Get. The. Fuck. Out," Eric said.

Ninety seconds later Stewart's bag went bouncing down the apartment complex stairs; Stewart bounded down ten seconds later, taking the steps two at a time, amscraying back to LAX, and Idaho. Eric watched from Kate's doorway as the fat man fled the courtyard, watched another twenty seconds to be sure that he was gone. The momentary scuffle faded into the night, replaced by the quiet trickling of the fountain. Like it never happened.

Back in Kate's doorway, Eric stood, pulse pounding. He had no earthly idea how he had done what he just did. It wasn't a move Eric intrinsically knew how to make; it was a move Matt Black did.

Eric heard a small noise behind him, turned to see Kate standing in the little kitchenette. He stepped back inside. She looked vulnerable and contrite.

"Is he gone?" she asked.

"He re-thought his itinerary," Eric replied.

Kate almost smiled at that, then something — sadness? — overtook her. She brought her hands up to her face, gave a little shudder. Then shook it off.

"Thank you," she said. She stepped forward a bit; soft light from the courtyard framed her through the window blinds, and in that moment she looked like a lost little girl — beautiful but wounded. Something pinged in Eric's chest; in the small confines of her apartment the air between them felt quietly but suddenly charged. Post conflict adrenaline rush, perhaps. Perhaps, something else.

"Uhm, I should probably go," Eric said softly.

Kate nodded. But as he turned toward the front door she reached out and softly touched his arm.

"Stay?" she asked.

ACT TWO

21.

A retro Felix the Cat clock hung on Kate's kitchen wall: google eyes shifting back and forth in synch with its curled plastic tail, as if it were privy to some winsome secret. The circular clock in its round black belly read little hand on three, big hand in twenty.

Kate lay on the sofa, clad in sweats and a spaghetti strap t-shirt, hands loosely folded across her chest, head on a little throw pillow. She was staring up at the ceiling. Refracted light from the pool played across its surface, casting softly undulating patterns. Eric sat on the floor near the sofa's edge, beside and behind her, one arm leaning into the sofa. The vibe was calmer now, but intensely intimate. They had been talking for several hours now — about life, love, the universe... everything but the obvious.

The moment between them went quiet.

"Ask a stupid question?" he said at last. She nodded.

"How did you meet that mook?"

Kate sighed.

"I was in a chat room," she confessed. "Pathetic, right? He said was divorced and had three kids, had his own house, and he worked for the government. Something high security. He seemed nice at first, told me everything I wanted to hear. But everything he said was a lie." A small, confessional laugh. "He's a security guard at a shopping mall. He lives in his mom's basement. And his 'kids'? He got their names from the chat room."

"Oh my God," Eric groaned, stifling a chuckle. "What a dick..."

"Tell me about it," Kate said. "Took me a week to figure it out. How blond of me..."

Eric sighed and shook his head; as he did he caught a fresh glimpse of her limber body stretched across the sofa. A breeze stirred outside, wafting the sheer drapes. Her nipples stiffened under the thin fabric of her tee. She wasn't wearing a bra. Eric looked away.

"It's not your fault," he told her. "How could you know?"

"I should by now," she countered. "It's hard to meet a decent guy. All the good ones are taken, I've been down that road before. And the rest..." she paused. "When I met Stewart at LAX, I was watching every guy who got off the plane. Then I saw him and thought, please God no, not him..."

Her thought trailed off. Kate stirred on the sofa, emotionally exhausted and starting to drift. Eric looked at her again, hearing her breathing shift into slumber; as she turned on her side her t-shirt rode up, revealing the soft curve on her back and hips.

Eric got up quietly. She looked peaceful, utterly beautiful. He reached over her and grabbed the little fuzzy sofa throw, laid it over her. As he did her hand drifted up to touch his.

"Thank you for tonight..." she said in a sleepy, soft voice. "Thank you for being... decent..."

Eric gave her hand a little squeeze, and Kate drifted off. He watched her for a moment longer.

Then, locking the door behind him, quietly let himself out.

22.

Always a bad sign when Marty Blumenthal paced rather than strolled through a notes meeting. Marty Blumenthal was not happy.

"Eric," he began. "The new draft…"

"You like?" Eric replied, poker facing it. Todd sat across the conference table, pen poised on notepad.

"Some brilliant stuff in there," Marty said. "But the penthouse scene…"

"Just trying to have some fun with it," Eric countered, heading him off. "Kind of The Grifters meets To Live and Die in LA…"

In the truncated hyper-speak A meets B by way of C of Hollywood, it was the kiss of death to reference movies old enough to saw in half and count the rings… hell, the 90's were an ice-age ago. Somehow Eric didn't care; they were great movies. His silence stood his ground.

"No I get it," Marty said. "Black does two chicks on a bed of money, what's not to like?

Eric nodded; indeed. "But Salma might play Trina," Marty continued, "she won't do girl-girl. And like I said, we move it to the beach house, we can use the same location…"

"Right," Eric scribbled on his pad.

"And that firebombing scene," Marty pressed on, "that's a shitload of CGI and green screen, plus the helicopter tracking shots. That's what… two-forty?" He glanced at Todd.

Todd checked his notes. "Two-eighty," he corrected.

"Two hundred and eighty thousand for one scene," Marty turned back to Eric. "We can't do that…"

"But you wanted that..." Eric replied, checking his own handwritten notes. "'Smoked glass shrapnel raining down like razored confetti on an unsuspecting city?' Like Cloverfield IV by way of 28 Months Later?"

Marty hated being quoted on things he had changed his mind about; it went against the flow. "I know," he said. "It's big. We need big. We just need it... smaller."

Marty smiled at Eric encouragingly. Eric scribbled notes and nodded.

"You got it," he said.

23.

It was almost seven as Eric stood at the gas grill by the pool, scorching boneless chicken breasts black. Not that he was trying to torture the food; his mind was just elsewhere. Paige was upstairs in the apartment; they had spoken less than ten words with each other. Emotional Stalingrad, and winter was upon them, in the warm Pacific sun.

"Hi neighbor!" Marin, cheery shuffling out in her bunny slippers to take in the sunset. "Whatcha making?"

"Uhm, food," Eric said, flipping the breasts with a spatula. "Or a mess…" he added, not wanting to seem overly blunt.

"Smells good!" Marin offered, and lit a cigarette.

Just then Kate came up the stairs from the parking garage on the far side of the complex. She was dressed in work scrubs — she had told him her job was a receptionist at a local plastic surgeon, the scrubs not so much a necessity as lending an air of *esprit de corps* to the position. But she looked adorable in them. Marin spied her just as Eric did.

"Hi Kate!" she called in full-on concierge mode.

Kate looked over, smiled and waved; then she saw Eric at the grill and shot him a quick smile. Eric smiled back, went back to grilling. But he watched her as she ascended the stairs. Even through the baggy scrubs he could see the curve of her backside. Girl had a heart-shaped ass. Eric felt his own heart skip a beat.

He looked away, happened to catch a glimpse of Marin. She'd picked up on it.

Eric cooked the chicken.

Back in the apartment, Eric and Paige dined in hollow domesticity: she paid bills online on her laptop as he pretended to watch the TV. But his thoughts were racing.

Eric had never cheated on a woman in his life; quite the opposite, he had long track record of being the guy women friends could talk to when their men were cheating. He was fluent in guy-speak but nakedly willing to bust out his half of the chromosome pool to thin the weasel herd, and he was wholly a one-woman man.

And this?

Nothing had 'happened'... technically speaking, anyway. He had stuck his nose in other peoples' business and ended up in fleeting hero of the moment mode to someone in trouble, which felt good. The fact that she was very beautiful and easy to talk to just sweetened it in the aftermath. But no moves were made. Naughty bits had not bumped in the night.

But still it felt by turns illicit, exciting, mysterious. Perhaps because of the absence of random gropings. And those feelings, while real, were all cheap thrills compared to what he really felt.

Alive. For the first time, in a very long time. Like a man coming back from a coma, or released from a tomb to smell fresh air. His libido was doing a low grade Lazarus, primordial stirrings shuffling through his senses.

Suddenly his cell phone vibrated in his pocket. He pulled it out, surreptitiously laid it on his thigh. Paige was staring at her laptop, forking chicken.

"Met with Marty today," he said to her, adding, "he has more notes."

"Uh-huh," Paige said absently, her attention pointedly elsewhere. "When's he going to pay you?"

Eric said nothing, looked down. There was a text, from Kate. It occurred to him, he'd scribbled his cell number on a Post-It and left it on her kitchen counter, on the off-chance of a Stewart resurgence. The text glowed on the LCD screen.

beach 2nite? It asked.

Eric thought about it for a moment, ate a forkful of food with one hand, his other tracing the contours of the numeric keypad.

y...e...s... he typed.

24.

It was almost midnight when Kate and Eric walked along the water's edge. They were close enough to touch, but did not. Low surf washed up and back in cascading rhythms. The moon hung full, fat and silver behind broken clouds, backlighting them and making the waves ripple and glow. The glittering crescent of the coastline arced before them. They were only two people on the moonlit shore, a pair of shadows to rest of the world. It felt brazen yet intimate, as if they were the only people in the world.

"…and then there was Richard," Kate told him, "married but rich. He said it wasn't about the sex with us, he just enjoyed the company. He was always polite, respectful. He used to like to take me places — Cabo, Vegas. One time he called me at the last moment and said, come with him to Spain for the week. I was like, Richard, I work…"

She gave a rueful little snort, brought one hand up to her mouth. It was girlish, endearing. "How long were you with him?" he asked.

"Two years, on and off," she replied.

"Why did you stop?"

"Easy," she said. "I got pregnant."

A beat of silence. "I've never told anyone that before," she confessed.

The moment was naked but strangely unguarded. "What did you do?" he asked, instantly thought, stupid question.

"What I had to," Kate replied, glancing out at the sea as if travelling in time. "He went golfing that day," she added. "But he paid for it."

"God…" Eric said.

They continued walking. Surf hissed onto sand. Eric reached out and touched her hand, then let go. A moment later, she took his hand in hers, gave it a little squeeze, and their fingers interlaced. It felt electric.

Just then Kate pointed out at the sea. "Look," she said.

Eric looked where she was pointing. The waves were glowing a soft bright blue as they curled and crested, as if lit from within.

"Oh my God," she said.

"Bioluminescence," he said. Kate looked at him; Eric continued awkwardly. "Algae in the water, the tide causes a chemical reaction. Look…" he nodded to their feet. Kate looked down; their bare footprints glowed in the wet sand. They looked back and saw their tracks glowing faintly, then erased by the next wave.

"It's beautiful," she said.

"Yeah," Eric replied. He was looking at her.

25.

Eric sat alone in the big leather pub chair in the imaginary living room of his imaginary beach house. The lights were off, the chair turned to afford a view of the crashing surf outside. He was barefoot, in jeans, no shirt, a bottle of pricey import beer in one hand. He could feel the cool of the bottle as he raised it to his lips, taste the malt and the hops as he swallowed a swig. His other hand traced a line up his lean torso to his neck, then up until his fingers were lost in his thick hair. He grabbed it, gave it a tug. His scalp hurt.

He knew he was in his little office, eyes heavy but focused as his other fingers clicked the laptop keys. But he could not feel the connection. He was here and here was real, in this moment. Eric gaze out at the waves.

"Stop," he said.

The waves froze in mid-curl. He closed his eyes, ran the curve of the bottle across his brow. "Glow," he whispered.

Eric opened his eyes: bioluminescence lit the halted surf, little imaginary marine dinoflagellates illuminating the sea.

"Go," he said, and the tide started again: waves crashing in obedience but following their own innate rhythms. Just then he heard something behind him.

"Baby?" A voice from behind him.

Trina had emerged, backlit from the bedroom doorway: long dark hair lustrous and thick, cascading down to cover her breasts. She was wearing his unbuttoned shirt and nothing else: though his back was to her Eric could see the cool lines and curves of her in his mind and smell the scent of her on his own skin.

"Away," he said.

Just like that, Trina was gone. The bedroom light went out. Eric sat in the expansive beamed room, alone, with only the glowing surf as company.

And then he was driving through the night, heading south on the 405 as it curved and hooked through Santa Monica. The sky was crystal clear, backwashed from the illumination of Century City and Hollywood beyond as Eric shifted and punched it, pressed the car past one hundred thirty… one forty… one fifty…

"Dark," he said, and the city lights winked out around him as he drove on, the only soul moving through the silent city of his mind.

26.

Eric sat in Gabe's office with his eyes closed, talking.
"I had this weird dream — I was floating over Hell, at the edge of the final abyss," he said. "And all these souls were crowded there. But the demons were just... businesslike. No whips or pitchforks."

In Eric's mind, the vast eternal abyss, black and swirling. Untold billions of lost souls crowded the ragged, craggy edge, their lemming faces withered, sparks of light smoldering in their empty eyes sockets. Demons moved among them, their faces malformed and hideous but clad in diabolical business attire like Wall Street sharks....

"The demons explained that you could toss yourself in any time you liked, and all your pain would disappear, along with everything else," Eric continued, eyes still closed. "But the last thing you'd see was the face of whomever you loved, winking out, forever."

In his mind, a doomed Eric huddled naked at the edge, the light in his own empty eyes. He watched as one lost soul, then another, pitched itself in, saw their howling faces as they disappeared. Others crowded at the rim, skeletal hands clawing at him and each other, desperate....

"They couldn't let go," Eric said. "The demons didn't need to torment them. They did that on their own, just fine."

Eric opened his eyes. "Hey, think I should write that sometime?" he asked.

"How are you and Paige these days?" Gabe asked. He looked concerned.

"Like a commercial for fake happiness," Eric snorted. "I'm

just a prop she uses to advertise her own success in life...like I'm a stray pound puppy she doesn't have the heart to put to sleep..."

"Everyone's the star of their own movie, Eric," Gabe noted. "Don't let yourself become a supporting player in someone else's drama."

"Yeah but how does that work in real life?" Eric asked. "What do you do when your life is a movie but you hate it?"

Gabe shrugged. "Re-write it?" he offered.

Silence. Eric just sighed and looked down. Gabe cocked his head quizzically.

"Is there something else you want to talk about?" he asked.

Eric looked up at him.

"No," he lied.

27.

It was late the next night when Eric met Kate under a streetlight on the Esplanade, near the closed and darkened lifeguard station. He had waited for Paige to drift off to sleep, minutes dragging on in dog years, the bedroom door ajar. He paused at the threshold, listening to the sound of her breathing. Then surreptitiously slipped out the front door.

The night was chilly and peaceful as he had walked down the hill, crossed PCH and made his way down one of the Avenues, tidy little seven figure cottages lining the street on either side, the residents tucked in slumber. He had felt a strange thrill. Like a man being bad. It felt good to be bad.

Kate was standing in the glow of a streetlight looking out at the sea as he arrived. They were near one of the deserted lifeguard stations, one of their agreed meeting places. She was wearing a hoodie and sweats, wisps of blond air delicately framing her face. She looked casually, crazily beautiful. Kate turned, saw him, and smiled.

"C'mon," she said, holding out her hand.

"Where are we going?" Eric asked.

They walked onto the jumbled angled horseshoe of the pier, the only two taking in the night air. Eric marveled at the grungy promenade as they passed the jutting octagonal turret of Old Tony's seafood restaurant, the silhouettes of partying locals visible through the windows of the upstairs bar.

"Wow, I've never been," he said, taking it in. "Feels more East Coast than LA."

"Tony's has been around since like 1952," Kate said. "My

mom used to model up there when she was young."

"Seriously?" Eric said.

"Yeah, like fashion shows and stuff," Kate replied. "Waaay back in the day." She gestured ahead. "And my grandpa would take me fishing here when I was little. Coming here always makes me feel good."

They stopped by a steel picnic table near one of the empty bait stations and stood at the rail, looking out at the waves pulsing toward the rocky inner beach. Kate grew pensive.

"What are you thinking?" Eric asked.

"I dunno. Dumb stuff...."

"Like?"

"Like I wish I could just jump in a funky old car with the top down and the wind in my hair," Kate told him. "Just... escape."

She gave a sad little laugh. "This isn't exactly how I thought my life would work out, you know? It's like I keep coming to the same point, over and over again, no matter what I do..."

Eric nodded. He knew the feeling.

"Sometimes I just feel so stupid," she said quietly. "So... ugly..."

"Hey..." Eric reached out to her. "Hey..."

Kate looked at him, eyes glistening. A solitary tear leaked out, tracking down one cheek. Eric traced a finger gently down her face, catching it before it fell. He held his finger up, her perfect teardrop balanced on the tip.

"You're beautiful," he told her.

She looked at him, eyes so wide he felt like he could see her soul. He moved incrementally closer then, the air space between them charged and sparking in the night air.

Eric kissed her. Soul soft, a silken caress of lips and breath.

Then Kate kissed him back.

Kate pressed Eric into the apartment wall, mouths and tongues searching with animal abandon. They pulled at each other's clothes, leaving them tangled on the floor. They could not get naked enough fast enough.

Eric marveled at her body, bathed in the moonlight: narrow waist over fecund hips, silver dollar nipples ripe and hard as they brushed against his chest. She bit his neck and Eric sprouted a hard-on the size of Florida. It bumped against her belly and Kate giggled, then went down to say howdy.

"Oh God," Eric gasped as she took him in her mouth. "Oh my fucking God…"

He hadn't been with another woman in ice ages, eons. He had forgotten what it felt like to be well and truly fucked. The carnal thaw flooded his senses then ignited him: liquid fire pulsing up his spine and radiating out through every pore. Eric sucked wind and something primal came out: a low growl from deep within. He pulled her up and picked her up, lowering her onto the sofa. Kate's legs came up and over his shoulders as she cocked her hips to afford him entry. And enter Eric did, sliding deep inside her. They both gasped.

And then the serious fucking began.

28.

The Felix the Cat clock read three fifteen by the time they stopped, little plastic feline eyes shifting to and fro, to and fro. Kate and Eric lay spent on the living room floor, bodies bathed in sweat and coital scent. As a lover Kate was nothing Eric had expected and everything he desired: sweet and dirty by turns, downshifting from slut to schoolgirl to holy sacred whore of Babylon in a heartbeat, gasping and giggling and completely, utterly uninhibited. They had fucked in every room and on every surface, in every position, a Kama Sutra home game made flesh. And in addition to her other attractive qualities, Kate was seemingly spontaneously multi-orgasmic, bucking and writhing and spurring him on with lips and hips and words and tongue, until he felt himself flowing over her falls, expending himself utterly. If she was faking it, it was world class, but he didn't feel like she was. It felt passionate and sensual, forbidden yet strangely pure. They fucked like two people trying to beat back lifetimes of sadness and solitude. Like it was the only clean thing in their messy lives.

The ceiling fan twirled lazily overhead as Eric lay on his back, watching. Kate laid her head on his chest, their bodies entwined. Eric traced one hand up her torso, fingertips describing skin hieroglyphs across the soft rise of her belly, the little folds at her waist. Kate shuddered and wiggled.

"That tickles," she said, shifting into him and adding, "I'm fat. I need to go to the gym..."

"Bullshit," he said. "You're perfect."

"I'm not in my twenties anymore," Kate said.

"So?" Eric countered. "You're the woman I want."

"What about your wife?" Kate asked suddenly, quietly.

Reality starkly intruded. Eric glanced over at the clock as Felix clocked time.

"It's over," he told her. "Has been for a while."

Kate gave another sad laugh. "Yeah," she said. "I've heard that before…"

"Not from me," Eric said, one hand stroking her hair. "I've never had 'an affair'. I just cashed in all my good guy chips."

"What are you waiting for?"

Eric thought about it. What, indeed.

"My movie," he told her. "My escape."

Kate said nothing. Eric sighed. "She wants it, too," he continued. "She doesn't think it will happen but she wants the money when it does. She needs it to feed her dream."

Kate sat up on one elbow, looked at him. "What do you need?" she asked.

Eric ran his hand up the line of her until he touched her face. And he kissed her again.

29.

Eric munched toast and sipped coffee at the kitchen table, morning sun glowing through the windows. It was seven forty. He'd had less than two hours sleep. He never felt better.

He rose as Paige emerged from the hallway, dressed for work. Eric placed a cup of tea and a hard-boiled egg and toast before her as she sat, then re-filled his mug and joined her. Breakfast at the Bests. Just another day.

Paige cracked her egg, decidedly unpleased. Eric said nothing.

"Where were you last night?" she finally asked.

"Went to the beach," Eric told her, sipping his coffee, completely nonplussed. "All the way to the pier."

"What do you do down there?"

"Walk. Think. Dream," he replied. "You're the one who wanted to move to the ocean. You should try it sometime."

"I have to work," Paige huffed. Then got up and got her stuff, heading for the door.

Eric munched his toast and watched her go. As the front door closed behind her he smiled.

"Don't we all..." he said.

30.

Back in the HOOYAH! hive Eric sat as his workstation, approving and declining away. Even this didn't bother him anymore. He was wracking up record numbers. As he worked his mind replayed the night with Kate over and over, each time drinking in a new detail. The sound she made when she came. The way her body moved to his touch. The way her touch made his soul shudder. How, in the moment before he first kissed her on the pier, a little voice in his head sounded.

If you kiss this woman, there is no going back...

And it was true, he knew. He couldn't imagine going back, or wanting to. He did not know what would happen next between he and Paige as their dead marriage finally twitched and went still. But whatever it was, it would mostly be a matter of paperwork and choreography. And timing.

The locus of his heart had shifted. Eric felt like a multiple amputee who had awakened to find his limbs restored. The phantom pain revealed itself as the tingling of nerves long thought dead.

Paige would not go lightly, he knew. Their marital chasm was consecrated by time and sickly perfected: a grim dance masking to the outer world as happy union. It occurred to Eric that, were the genders reversed, no one would question the nature of their dynamic.

Abuse, Eric thought. Emotional abuse...

But he wasn't a victim. He would no longer have his own concerns hijacked and turned against him. He had taken it for years, in the hope it might change, that things might get better.

But Eric no longer cared. He had other things to think about.

Better things. Like a new life, unbound by bitter recrimination. A new future, as yet unwritten.

And the possibility of love...

Eric's cell vibrated on the desk. An incoming text. It was from Kate.

It read, Luv U.

Eric smiled. He texted back.

Luv U 2.

31.

Paige and Eric were in the checkout line at Trader Joe's when his cellphone rang. Eric paused in the midst of pulling groceries out of the cart and looked at the phone, mouthed the word Marty at her, then stepped outside, leaving her to finish.

"Hello..." Eric said, stalking the thimble-sized parking lot and moving toward Paige's SUV.

"Eric, I have Martin for you..." Todd, dutifully patching him through. Marty's voice came a moment later, scratchy and distorted.

"Eric, I'm in the hills but I had a flash..." The call glitched and came back. "...the garage scene....I like it but let's give it a twist..."

"Twist?" Eric asked, speaking too loud and feeling stupid for it. Marty continued.

"A double cross... something to keep the audience jumping... big shootout maybe...."

Eric rolled his eyes. Bad transmission, wind noise. He could picture Marty, snaking through the Hollywood Hills in his Benz with the top down, Bluetooth glued to his ear, dispensing cinematic wisdom like a burning bush.

"Explosion..." Marty's voice was phasing out. "Blow the fuck out of..."

The call went dead. Eric turned and saw Paige coming out, pushing the cart, looking peeved. He started putting the bags in the back.

"What did he want?" Paige asked.

"He had a flash," Eric replied.

"Uh-huh," Paige snorted. "Is he going to pay you yet?"

Back at the Seascape courtyard, Eric and Paige lugged grocery bags in. Other tenants were in the pool, hanging out in the courtyard. Eric glanced up and saw Marin on her stoop, all fuzzy slippers and sweats, box wine and smokes. She waved.

As they crossed the courtyard another door opened: Kate, exiting her apartment with a basket of laundry. She saw Eric and smiled, then saw Paige and didn't, heading down the stairs to the laundry room, and away. Paige picked up on it instantly.

"You know her?" she asked Eric.

"That's Kate," Eric replied. "The neighbor."

"You've met?" Paige continued.

"Couple of times," Eric answered, deflecting. "She's nice."

"That's not what I heard," Paige sniffed. "Marin said she drinks and sleeps around. Bob calls her 'the whore in thirty-four.'"

"Marin and Bob are idiots," Eric said.

Just then they heard a whoop and looked up to see Bob, in board shorts and sunglasses, drunk as a monkey and tottering up the second floor stair railing. He balanced precariously, whooped again, and jumped, barely landing in the pool and missing a neck-snapping concrete face-plant by inches. Eric glanced at Paige.

"I rest my case," he said.

Eric unpacked the bags the grocery bags as Paige changed into gym clothes, though still wearing full makeup. Minutes had passed but she emerged from the hallway as if the conversation were seamless.

"That's not the point," she said.

"What's not what point?" Eric asked.

"I don't like her," Paige declared, packing her gym bag.

"Who?"

"Her. The neighbor," she replied.

"You don't like anybody," Eric said. "You don't even like Marin…"

"You know what I mean," Paige countered. "I don't want you talking to her. Do you understand me?"

And there was something in that tone that rankled Eric at his core. She wasn't speaking to him as a husband or mate or partner, however alienated. She was talking to him like an underling. A misbehaving servant.

He had thought about it and decided, whatever happened, he would not lie. Withhold information, be less than totally forthcoming... fair game, in their toxic dance. But lie? No.

Her question hung in the air. Eric pulled a beer from the freshly stowed groceries, popped the can. He looked at her.

"Perfectly," he said. He took a sip as Paige waited expectantly.

"And?" she said.

Eric smiled sweetly.

"How can I put this?" He set the beer down and leaned in to her. "Nobody tells me whom I can and can not talk to," he replied. "Ever."

Eric leaned closer for emphasis.

"Not even you..."

Paige said nothing. Eric sipped his beer. Something about him had changed, gone harder, stronger. Calm, but kind of scary. Not like Eric. More like, Matt Black.

Paige backed off. Took her gym bag.

And headed for the door.

32.

Back in scriptworld Eric stood in the center of the fourth floor of a deserted parking structure, a sleek metal attaché case upright by his leg. He was dressed entirely in black, eyes fixed on the up ramp. He couldn't see Toad or Trina. That was precisely the point.

From the third floor came the hum of engines; a moment later headlights illuminated the ramp. Eric stood his ground as two hulking black SUVs gunned up the ramp, heading straight toward him. Some fifty feet away they parted, pulling into opposing parking slots. Eric watched as the doors opened and a dozen swarthy goons stepped out, assuming wary flanking positions. Then the shotgun door of the second SUV opened, and Tio lumbered out. He was a hulking East Euro heavy in tailored Armani, all thick jowls and stubble and grim Slavic smile, and straight out of central casting. Tio sized Eric up.

"Mister Black," he said in a guttural boom. It sounded like Meestah Blahk. "You have my package?"

Eric nudged the attaché; it fell over by his feet, a heavy echo reverberating through the structure. "Got mine?" he answered.

Tio nodded to his crew. One goon produced a black duffel bag and placed it on the ground near Tio; Tio nodded and the goon unzipped it and gave it a hefty push.

The bag slid across the concrete, stopped neatly before Eric. He glanced down and saw thick bundles of cash stuffed inside.

"You want to count?" Tio called out, "Or you trust me?"

"No," Eric said. He shoved the attaché with one foot; it slid over to Tio, stopped movie-perfect at Tio's feet.

Duffel goon knelt down to open the case. No go. "Locked," he said.

Tio scowled, and growled in thick Slavic tongue. "Nee pees deet Black. Don't fuck with me. What's the combination?"

Tio glared, completely unaware of small red point of light glowing in the middle of his expansive back, then gliding up to the base of his skull. A laser dot.

Eric smiled grimly. Completely unaware of a second dot, gliding up his own.

"Three two one," Eric said pleasantly.

Tio nodded to the goon, who clicked the combination on the latch. Three… two… one…

The latch popped free. The goon opened the case.

BOOOOOM! Smoke and flame belched forth as the case blew, wounding Tio and killing half his men in a heartbeat as a shockwave wracked the structure and a hail of returning gunfire sent bullets pinging everywhere. The fire reached one of the SUVs, which began to burn.

Toad and Trina opened fire from the shadows as Eric dove and rolled and came up shooting, a Glock in each hand, killing with kinetic economy. If this were real life he'd have missed everything and been shot fifty times, deaf and scorched and riddled with shrapnel.

But this was scriptworld, and Matt Black was its reigning Lord of Death. Eric spun and dropped another goon just a maimed Tio opened up with a Tec 9 on full auto; as he did Time skewed and Eric saw the cartridges falling in glittering cinematic slo-mo. Eric dove behind a pylon and chucked his spent magazines and one Glock, slapping a fresh mag into the other as the Tio advanced, hacking connect-the-dots divots out of the concrete leading to…

…Eric, who came up blasting, sending Tio into a spastic jittering death jig, the big man shuddering with each hit before dropping with a dull splat.

Eric stood in the carnage, adrenalized and grimly victorious. Then he saw a shadow move from the corner of his eye; as he turned he saw a muzzle flash.

And a bullet zoomed straight for his head.

"STOP!" Eric yelled.

The bullet halted in mid-air, pointing dead at him, still spinning. Eric looked around at the frozen firefight in play all around him. "Who shot Black? he yelled. "Who fucking shot Black?"

Eric whirled. "Toad shot Black?" he yelled. Then he saw Toad, hunkered on the next level, his weapon in mid-flare as he popped a random goon.

"Trina shot Black?" He turned again and saw Trina, frozen as she fell back from a bullet in the shoulder: the kind of wound which in real life would usually mean shock, unconsciousness and death from blood loss but in movies required only a CUT TO and a costume change.

Eric was furious, confused. He had no idea where this had come from. He turned back to the mystery bullet, still spinning in the air before him as if awaiting further instruction. Eric lashed out and slapped it, knocking it harmlessly to the concrete…

… then screamed FUCK! as he clutched his hand in pain.

And then Eric was back in his office, sitting at his desk, temples thudding from a skull-crushing headache.

"Fuck…" he echoed. He brought a hand up to his temples, winced. "What the…"

Eric stared in shock at his palm. And the angry red of a bullet-shaped burn etched there.

33.

There was a knock at the front door of Unit 34. Kate answered to find Eric: urgent, excited, more than a little crazed.

Kate let him in, closed the door behind him. Eric entered and saw the kitchen counter glowing from a half dozen candles, heard a sad iTunes love song playing on repeat in the background. There was a jumbo bottle of Chardonnay near the candles. It was almost empty.

"Kate, I need to talk to you," Eric said, hugging her.

"Sure," she replied, pulling away. "I need to talk to you, too." There was a wine glass in her hand. It was almost empty, as well. Eric released her and Kate sauntered over to the kitchen counter, refilling her glass. Then she went to the sofa and sat. Eric kneeled beside her.

"Let me ask you something completely insane," he began. "If your dream came to life and you could escape into it, would you?"

"What?"

"Baby, I don't know how it happened but mine did," Eric told her. "And I can."

"You can what?" Kate asked. She took another swig and set the glass down on the coffee table.

"Go there," Eric blurted. "Be there. I don't know how, but..."

"What are you talking about?" she asked.

"My movie," Eric said. "It's real..."

"Wait... your movie is getting made?" she asked, trying to wrap her brain around it.

"Not yet..." Eric said, fumbling. "I mean, not the one I'm making, the one I made. The one in my mind..."

This was not going well. Kate was totally lost; she waved her hand in frustration and stood, reaching down to grab her glass. It was only then that Eric noticed exactly how lit she was. As she went to pour another he followed, uncomfortably aware that he sounded crazy.

"Eric, you're starting to freak me out," Kate said. She emptied the dregs of the bottle in her glass.

"I know it sounds nuts, but look…" Eric said, then held up his palm to show her the burn. "I wrote it, it happened there, and I brought it back."

"Eric, please…" Kate was visibly impatient, agitated. She moved around him, out of the little kitchenette. On her computer, the sad song was re-playing; Kate clicked the mouse, scrolling down to another. "Just, stop."

"You have to believe me — my script came to life and now I'm living it! And it was good, but now it sucks…" He took her in his arms. "…'cuz you're not there."

Eric hugged her. Kate did not hug back; quite the opposite, her body felt pliant but hollow. Like hugging a shadow. Or a ghost. "What's wrong?' he asked.

"I can't handle this," she told him, stiffening. "Any of it."

Kate pulled away and went back to the computer, started absently scrolling the screen. And that was then Eric saw what else was on the monitor.

"Christ," he muttered. "You're back in the chat rooms?"

"I'm just looking!" Kate said defensively. "God! I'm just trying to figure some things out, okay?"

She abandoned the computer and went to the counter, grabbing the empty wine bottle. "Shit," Kate hissed, and fished another out of the fridge. Eric watched as she corkscrewed it open, poured an angry glass. Whatever was happening here did not begin with his bizarre confession.

"Kate, talk to me," he said. "What's wrong?"

"Everything," she replied. "All of it." She paused.

"Richard called," she said flatly. "He wants to take me to Italy. Some business trip."

Eric felt some inner trapdoor open, an emotional noose tightening around his throat. A cold anger flushed through him.

"Wait… rich-married-asshole-Richard?" he said. "I'll-go-golf-while-you-scrape-my-kid-out Richard??"

"I don't care who takes me where," Kate answered bitterly. "And you have no room to talk."

She slugged the wine back defiantly. Eric had never seen this side of her, the cold ugly edge of it. "What?" he asked. "What the fuck does that mean?"

"You're married, Eric!" she spat back. "I told you I won't go down that road again!"

"But you'll go to Italy with rich married Richard?"

Kate laughed. "At least it's not here," she said, toasting the air. She drained the glass and smacked it on the counter, then tried to walk away. Eric stopped her.

"He doesn't love you," Eric said. "I do. And you love me!"

"No," Kate said. "I don't. I can't." She shook her head, looked away.

"I won't."

Eric took her and kissed her then, pulling her into him. Something seemed to melt in her, and for a moment Kate gave in to it. Then she stiffened again and pushed him away.

"Would you just go?" she said. "Get out of here, Eric…"

"Kate, no…"

"Just GO!" her voice came up. "Get OUT of here!!"

Kate grabbed the empty wine glass and hurled it past him. It smashed on the wall. Eric held both hands up in mute supplication.

"GO!!!" she cried.

Eric backed off, leaving her wavering in the living room.

As he exited, he could hear her start to cry.

34.

Just like that... Eric kept thinking. Just like that.

It was the next day as he sat at his workstation, near the end of his shift, robotically processing search terms while his mind churned. Just like that, his life had gone from moribund to magical; just like that, his heart had gone from atrophied to alive again. And just like that, it had all ended.

He had fallen in love with a beautiful but deeply damaged woman; he had grasped at that love like a life ring to a drowning man, and it had buoyed him. And now his love was there but the woman was gone, and he felt himself slipping, sinking.

Just then Gillian strolled by, saw him stopped. "Eric, can you see me after you log out for the day?" she said.

"Sure thing," Eric told her.

It was six minutes later when Eric seated himself in Gillian's office. Gillian sat behind her desk, tapping on her keyboard and looking at her monitor. Her black hair sported threads of a new shade of blue today. He'd asked if she wanted the door closed and she'd said no, leave it open.

Gillian studied figures on the screen and nodded, impressed. "Over two thousand today..." she said.

"Twenty one-sixty," Eric offered. "I think I'm getting the hang of this..."

"Eric," Gillian paused, sighed a bit. "We've decided to give the perm slot to another candidate."

Eric was floored. "But I thought... you said... my scores..." He was babbling.

"Your scores are great," Gillian told him. "It's the tardies and absences. You disappeared in the middle of a shift, Eric. And we know you've been working on outside projects on company time…"

She reached over and produced a file, slid it across the desk. His workstation log. Eric saw fragments of his script in the keystroke report.

"Technically, that's against policy," Gillian continued. "Perms have a little latitude, but temps… we can't have that, Eric. I'm sorry."

Eric went pale as it dawned on him what was really happening here.

"Wait," he blurted. "You're canning me?'

Gillian went corporate efficient then, clearly not enjoying it. "I like you, Eric," she told him. "But your contract is up, and they decided not to renew." She paused. "I can write you a letter of recommendation…"

"This is bullshit!"

Eric snapped then, standing so fast the little ergonomic chair banged into the wall, loud. Gillian was taken aback. Other workers peered in through the big glass windows, witnesses to the execution.

Eric stood for a moment like his head would explode.

Then he stormed out.

35.

"You got fired??"

Paige was pacing before him as he sat at the kitchen table, already dressed in her gym clothes, furious. It was evening. Eric was in hell.

"My contract was up," Eric explained flatly. "They didn't renew."

"That's just great, I knew this was going to happen," Paige said, her tone acid. "Do you have another job lined up?"

"I have a job," Eric told her. "I have to finish the script."

Paige went ballistic. "I'm sick of this, Eric!" she wailed. "No one else would put up with it!" She stalked the living room, packing her gym bag. "There are a lot of guys who'd love to go out with me, you know..."

"Maybe you should," Eric said. Suddenly something clicked. "Wait... did you?"

Paige kept packing the bag, as the vibe went suddenly evasive and righteous.

"Did you?" Eric asked again.

It occurred to him even as he asked, he didn't really care — not in any testosterone-driven territorial imperative, anyway. He just wanted to know. He looked at her, head cocked quizzically, eyes fiercely focused. His gaze bored into her like a taunt; Paige squirmed defiantly in the heat of it.

"Don't look at me like that," Paige spat back. "I know what you've been doing, hanging out with that drunken slut who doesn't have a brain in her head."

"And what have you been doing?" Eric countered. "At the gym every night?"

Paige said nothing. Her silence spoke volumes. Eric smiled. It was too perfect.

"Of course, makes sense," he said. "Nice guy?"

A pause. Their eyes met. "He's very nice," she told him. "He thinks I'm beautiful. He wants to be with me…"

"And did you?" Eric stood from his place at the table. "'Be' with him?"

Paige drew back a bit. "We had coffee," she said.

"You don't drink coffee."

"Okay, a glass of wine," she amended. "At his place. He has a house on the peninsula. He's a normal guy…"

Eric just shook his head, chuckling ruefully. He started to walk away. Paige was defiant.

"You have nothing to say to me?"

Eric stopped. Looked at her.

"I'm sure you'll be very happy together," he said.

36.

The plasma light atop the bookshelf did its silent Frankenstein crackle as Eric stared through his office window. Paige was off to the gym and whatever, he was alone. Just then he caught glimpse of Kate heading out with a weekend bag, dressed for success. She paused on the far walkway and chatted with Bob and Marin on their stoop, smiling and sunny. Then she bopped down the stairs and was gone, too.

Eric stood for a moment, staring at the bookshelf, the light, the framed photos of himself in happier times. Then with one arm, he swept them all clattering to the floor.

Two hours later and the laptop keys clicked like crazed castanets. Eric's eyes were bloodshot and boring into the words flowing onto the screen. He was writing in a fugue state, willing himself into the story. And bending it to his will.

Paige had not come back from the gym; something told him she might not come home tonight at all. He didn't care. His real life was collapsing all around him. He could not change that. But he could change this.

And change he did: inserting Kate into the script, making it live and breathe her. At least, the parts of her he wanted. Eric scraped off the crazy and fed only the angels of her better nature in the mix: idealizing her, rendering the character erotic, empathetic, tuning her to his desire...

...and as he wrote the shower in the beach house roared, clouds of steam billowing forth as a wet and naked Trina became Kate, pulling Eric in...

...and Trina pushed Eric onto the penthouse bed, the other

woman and piles of money evaporating as Trina became Kate, her blonde hair loose and tousled as she crawled astride him and kissed his face and neck and chest, lips hot and soft, tongue darting...

And Eric was a god of this private universe, with the power to create and re-create to suit his needs as he wrote, and wrote, and wrote...

...and he was walking up the perfect beach toward Kate, who stood by water's edge, staring out at the waves. The last vestiges of the moon broke through obsidian clouds. As he neared Kate turned to him: fragile, haunting, ethereally beautiful. She enfolded him in her embrace, pulling him close.

"I'm sorry," she said. "I'm so sorry..."

Then she pulled him down to make love on the sand...

Eric came to and came back sometime the next day. He looked at what he had written, and emailed it to Marty. When he came out of his office the apartment was quiet and still. He peered into the bedroom — the bed was unslept in.

In the kitchen he found a note from Paige folded on the big pine table. Eric picked it up, read it. It announced that, apart from hating him with the heat of ten thousand white hot suns, she was leaving him, and she hoped he both rotted and burned in Hell sometime very soon. She seemed quite sure that God Almighty concurred with her in this.

Eric dropped the note where he found it. He had no idea what God thought, about anything.

But as he would discover, even a lesser god answered to a higher authority.

37.

"**E**ric what the fuck is this?"

Eric sat at his usual spot at the conference table as Martin not paced but stalked the room. He was decidedly unpleased, and when he was he transformed from 'Marty' to 'Martin'. An instantaneous dropping of the room temperature. A prelude to full blown histrionics. Todd looked down at his note pad, keeping his head down. Copies of the new draft lay on the table like paper lepers. Martin picked one up.

"I ask you for twists, and you give me a whole new fucking character?" He threw the script back down in disgust.

Eric held his ground. "I think it's good," he said. He slipped the little flash drive out of his pocket, began twirling it in his fingers under the table.

"Good?" Martin exclaimed. "It's a goddamned soap opera! And who the fuck is 'Kate'? This totally blows casting and takes the whole movie in a whole different direction!"

"I like it," Eric said, quietly pressurizing. "It's my script."

"Your script," Martin said. "My fucking movie. The studio is interested. They want to bring in another writer. I haven't shown this to 'em yet, 'cuz I'm fighting for you. But you gotta change it."

"But it's good," Eric insisted. "It's real..."

"Jesus!" Martin gazed to the ceiling as if invoking deities. "People don't wanna see 'real', Eric — they want 'real' they can see that for free!"

Martin downshifted then, became 'Marty' again, cosseting the temperamental artist. "I'm telling you, buddy," he advised Eric, strolling behind him and leaning in. "Trust me on this one.

Lose the chick. Change it back. Make it good again. Okay?"

It wasn't really a question. Martin had spoken and that was it. Done deal. He waited for the obligatory 'you got it' from Eric, and clapped him on the shoulder in ersatz camaraderie.

And that was when Eric exploded.

"Son of a BITCH!" Eric stood so fast he knocked the chair away, getting right up in Marty's grill. "You sanctimonious facile bastard!"

Eric glared at Marty. He didn't look temperamental or difficult. He looked dangerous. He grabbed one of Marty's awards — a fat glass obelisk, some cable company accolade, best remake of an adaptation of a sequel, or something — and heaved it at the glass conference room wall. The entire wall disintegrated on impact, glittering safety frags raining down and bouncing on the carpet.

Martin and Todd were stunned silent. For one fleeting moment, Eric owned the room.

Then he fled.

38.

Police car light bars were strobing as Eric pulled up in front of the Seascape Apartments. Two units, head to head in the dusk-tinged street. Eric parked and jumped out as two officers emerged through the courtyard. He hurried up, trying to appear nominally casual. He had a bad feeling.

"Officers, what's going on?" he asked. "I live here..."

One of the cops — 30s, female, Hispanic — sized him up. "Domestic disturbance," she told him. "It's over now."

Eric nodded and continued past them. Inside the courtyard, tenants peered from doorways like vultures; others murmured furtively around Trudy, the pretty, divorced single mom building manager. She rarely came to the building, but had been called in to defray the drama. She cast a sideways glance to Eric, who looked away.

Bob and Marin were at the top of the stairs; Eric came up, his tome hushed and urgent. "What the hell happened?" he asked.

"Dude, it was intense," Bob said. "She was freaking, man..."

Marin stepped in, the hostess with the mostest. "Kate lost it," she told him. "She started smashing things in her apartment, then she came over and was banging on your door."

"Yeah man, she was crazy wasted..." Bob interjected. He seemed inordinately pleased, just on general principal. Eric glanced back, saw Trudy eyeing him reproachfully through the crowd. He looked back at Marin.

"Where did she go?"

"She was really upset," Marin blurted. "Trudy is, too..."

"Where?" Eric hissed, intensity radiating off him like a blast zone.

Marin and Bob just cringed. From the courtyard, heads turned in their direction. Eric felt pinioned by the many gazes. Then he fled there, too.

39.

Déjà vu is a funny thing — that strange sensation that you'd not just seen but lived a moment before. Usually fast and fleeting, a moment within the moment that feels too familiar, and the very moment you realize it, it begins to fade. But tonight it only grew stronger, like a rip tide, sucking Eric in and under. Reality unraveled at the edges, rendering everything dream-like... and nightmarish.

Night had fallen as Eric screeched his car into the empty parking lot at the end of Esplanade and wracked the steering wheel, fat tires squealing as the car whipped around. Headlights illuminated the low blue-stained wooden fence at the edge of the lot as he threw open the driver's door and climbed out, the engine still rumbling. The cold glimmering Pacific churned surf at water's edge before him; he saw the twinkling black rocky hook of the Palos Verdes foothills to the south, the sweep of Esplanade as it hugged the beach to the north. But the lights of Malibu were obscured by a thick mass of encroaching marine layer, in the middle distance almost swallowing the tip of the pier. Down on the sand, the deserted lifeguard station stood like a sentinel.

She wasn't here. Something was wrong. He could feel it, and it filled him with a dull knife pang of dread. It radiated out from his gut as Eric speed-dialed his cellphone.

"C'mon, pick up..." he hissed. The call flipped to voicemail.

"Hi, if you want me, you know what to do.... " The throaty laugh. The annoying beeeep.

Somehow he knew what would happen next. He had to stop it.

Eric jumped back in his car and gunned it down the street.

40.

The pier was largely deserted, though Eric could hear 80's rock and roll thudding from the smattering of dive bars and the turret at Old Tony's… and under that, the ceaseless drone of pounding surf. Misty tendrils of fog clung to the light posts and hung in the night air.

Eric moved quickly, eyes darting as he scanned in every direction for some sign. As he cleared the last shop the outer pier opened up, waves pushing passed massive barnacled pylons, churning toward the rocky strip of inner beach. He saw the faded mural of whale and dolphins painted on the concrete. And then as the feeling of overwhelming dread spread from his gut to the pores of his skin, he saw it.

Her purse. Abandoned near the railing. Near the bait station.

But just beyond that he saw Kate, by the rails staring out at the water, talking into her cell phone.

"Kate!" he called out. She looked back and saw him with tear-stained eyes: she was drunk, disheveled, and way too far away.

"Kate, don't!" he cried.

But it was too late: Kate smiled a tragic smile, then climbed up on the railing and jumped.

"No…" Eric gasped, stomach twisting into his throat. "NO!!"

He peered over the rail into blackness, three foot waves smashing past pylons that loomed like the legs of dark giants, the water inky and foam flecked…

…then her head popped up, gasping for breath in the trough between waves, looking like a drowning cat. Her arms broke surface and flailed as she sputtered. Then another wave hit, and she was under.

Back on the pier, Eric freaked as Time both sped up and slowed again, a thousand thoughts racing through his mind in a microsecond as he stripped off his jacket and dialed 911 on his cell.

"There's a woman in the water off the pier!" he yelled into his phone. "She jumped!" He looked down and saw her head bob back up between waves; she was conscious, flailing.

"SWIM!!" he called out to her. "SWIM with the waves!!"

Eric could hear sirens from the police substation and fire department splitting the night. Then another wave hit, and she went under again.

"Fuck!" Eric dropped the cell, climbed on the rail, and jumped.

And in the ensuing rush of time and careening black space Time glitched, a mad hiccup in the flow of linear space and reason...

... as Eric hit and pierced the water's surface, fought his way back up through current and cold. The brine, the seaweed, the clammy taint of dead fish, the slimy trace of diesel and oil in the water... he clawed through the water, reaching for her...

...and Time glitched again and he was falling: the same sensations of the jump, the water, the sinking, the unmitigated terror and desperation. A wave filled his mouth as he backwashed into the pilings, all raw pain and deathly cold as heavily crusted barnacles rent his flesh, chewing him up. He tasted his blood in the merciless sea...

...Time glitched again and Eric hit the water, the sting of the surf like ten thousand needles injecting him with oblivion. His body seized up as his nervous system short-circuited, limbs leaden and adrift, throat constricting as his heart pounded mad counterpart to his heaving, oxygen starved lungs. And as she flailed the waves pulled him down, and Eric sank, his last thought a tortured, terrified NO...

And then it was dawn again. Chill. Grey. Desolate. The déjà vu feeling had evaporated, leaving only cold brute reality in it wake. Eric stood on the rocks lining the inner beach, listening to her voicemail for the thousand time.

"Eric I do love you," it said. "I'm so sorry... Forgive me..."

Eric lowered the phone. "What have I done?" he croaked. "What have I done?"

He stood alone, unshaven, sunken-eyed and dry. A little harbor boat putted, casting hooked long lines into the water.

He had never gone in. She had never come out.

And that was that.

ACT THREE

41.

Gabe listened to the message. Eric had just fessed up about Kate, the affair... everything but his forays into scriptworld. He held the cellphone out, letting it play.

"I'm so sorry," it repeated. "Forgive me..."

Gabe was shocked. "Eric, I'm so sorry..." he began.

"Yeah, lotta that going 'round," Eric said, low and devastated. "Know what's weird? Cops said, some jumpers wash up. Some never do. Some end up an all you can eat seafood buffet. You're the seafood."

The gallows humor crumbled. A moment later Eric did, too — head in hands, voice cracking.

"Oh god," he murmured. "It's all my fault..."

"No," Gabe told him. "It's not. You didn't do this, Eric. We all —"

Eric interrupted. "Gabe I love ya but I swear to God if you say the movie thing again my head'll explode..."

He sat up in his chair, grimly wiping tears away. He looked like a man on the edge, but steely now. Gabe sat back, watching.

"I was gonna say, choices," Gabe continued. "We all make 'em. We all have to live with 'em."

"Yup," Eric acknowledged, sighing grievously, reigning it all in. "Yup..."

An uncomfortable pause. "So what are you gonna do now?" Gabe asked at last.

Eric thought about it a moment. Then stood up. Shook Gabe's hand.

And left.

42.

When Eric arrived back at his apartment he happened upon Trudy, who was taping an envelope to his door with red duct tape. She didn't see him coming.

"Hi Trudy," Eric began, eyeing the envelope. Trudy looked at him, surprised at his sudden presence on the walkway.

"Eric, hi," she said, smiling uncomfortably. She was very pretty, golden blonde and sunny, an inveterate artist and California beach girl who'd lucked into steady sinecure managing several buildings for the owners, and he'd always liked her. But it was clear she hated this part of the job.

"Eric, I'm sorry," she said. The envelope wavered in the breeze. Then she took a breath, strapped on her game face. "The owners want the problem tenants gone…"

"Am I a 'problem tenant'?" Eric asked.

"No…" she said, then amended, "Well, it's just everything going on around here. We can't have that…"

She stopped, let it hang. "I'm really sorry," she concluded.

And with that, Trudy eased past him and headed down the stairs. Eric watched her go, then plucked the envelope from the surface of the door. He opened it.

An eviction notice.

43.

Eric entered the darkening apartment. The plasma TV was gone, as was most of the furniture. Paige had been a busy girl.

Eric tossed the envelope on the kitchen counter, searched through the cupboards. They were bare, freshly denuded. A few empty cardboard boxes and newspapers were scattered about, attesting to the work-in-progress exodus of it all.

Eric opened the freezer, saw a bottle of Stoli tucked in the back. A special occasions bottle, largely reserved for guests. He grabbed it, found a leftover glass, poured three finger's worth. He held the glass up, gazed through the refractions from the window's dying light.

"Good enough for Matt Black," he said. "Good enough for me."

Eric slugged it back. Felt the burn sluicing down to his guts. Then poured himself another.

44.

Once again he felt the surreal slither from unconsciousness to identity, drifting from darkness through strange and discomfiting dreams to naked awareness. He was unmoored from his body but felt himself settling in, like a creature crawling back into a uncomfortable but familiar skin cocoon. I AM... he thought... I AM...

Eric opened his eyes. He was sitting alone on edge of the low slung bed in the beach house, his bare feet touching the wide planked floor. But now he was not clad in the ersatz form of an imaginary guy named Matt Black, nor any hipper cooler version of himself. He was just, Eric. His clothes were his own, rumpled and careworn, slept in. His body ached, every cell awakening and hyper-aware. The last he remembered he had been writing, the bottle of vodka almost empty at his desk in some similarly strange place called the Seascape Apartments. But he was not drunk, no pangs of hangover plagued his aging flesh. Eric looked around the room.

No coy trail of lacy undergarments beckoned. The bedroom door was open, the house beyond eerily silent. As if awaiting his next move.

Eric stood on unsteady legs, made his way to the door. Then he heard that all-too familiar gurgling sound.

In the kitchen, no handy henchman nor sultry sirens awaited him: just the sleek and expensive Krups, dutifully making java. Eric reached out, felt the heat of it on his fingertips. Then he heard a sigh-soft sound coming from the living room: a barest stirring of the air. Eric felt suddenly light-headed and a whole body rush flooded him, prickling his skin.

He went to the doorway, peered in. The dizziness increased, his eyes tearing up. On the couch he caught glimpse of a diffuse shadow figure seated. Eric blinked, trying to focus, blinked again.

Then the rush passed. The figure coalesced into form.

And he saw her.

Kate was seated on the sofa, wearing a bathrobe, her hair swept back and damp. She was staring out at the sea through the massive windows.

"Kate?" he said softly. She looked at him, her expression faraway, spacey.

Eric rushed forward, embraced her as though afraid she would disappear if he let her go. Kate hugged him back as Eric smelled and felt her presence: not the perfect, idealized movie version Kate. Just, real.

And there.

"I had a weird dream," she said softly. "I was drowning, and you were calling my name…"

Eric said nothing, just hugged her even tighter. Kate laughed a little, squirming in his grasp.

"Baby, what's wrong?" she asked. "You okay?"

"Yes. Nothing…" he murmured. "Are you okay?"

"I'm fine," she replied. "Just a weird dream…"

Eric pulled back and gazed deeply into her eyes, his hands running through her damp locks. "Why is your hair wet?" he asked.

"Just took a shower, goofy…" she said. "I made coffee. Want some?"

She got up, heading for the kitchen. Eric watched, stunned. Then he followed.

He had no idea what was happening now, or how. Kate poured him a steaming mug and slid it across the big granite counter, then sipped from her own. As Eric watched Kate it was evident: she had even less. She was simply in this world, and it was all there was. But she was aware he was looking at her very, very strangely.

"What's going on?" she asked, suddenly self-conscious. "You're acting really weird..."

"I'm fine," he said. "I just really love you..."

"Awww," she smiled and came to him, gave him a big, sweet kiss. "I love you too, Eric..."

She started to walk away. He stopped her. "What did you call me?" he asked.

"Uhm, Eric... your name?" She looked at him askance. "Are you sure you're okay?"

Eric hugged her again, beaming. Kate giggled.

"I'm great," he told her, then, "Let's go somewhere. Today..."

Kate brightened. "Santa Barbara?" she asked.

"Bigger," Eric said. "Spain... Tahiti..."

"What?" Kate was bowled over.

"Let's just jump on a plane and go!" Eric continued. "Anywhere we want. It could be like a honeymoon..."

Kate's turn to be stunned. Her eyes suddenly glistened. "Are you... proposing?" she asked.

Eric suddenly felt something in his hand, not there the moment before. A small velvet box. He held it up like a magic trick, placed it in Kate's hands. Kate opened it and gasped at an exquisite engagement ring — not gaudy or stupidly huge but delicate and glittering. She was speechless as Eric took her hand.

"Marry me, baby," he said. "We can do it on a beach in Bali or with Elvis in Vegas, I don't care. Just be with me. Forever..."

Eric took the ring out of the box, slipped it on her finger. It fit perfectly.

"My God," she whispered. "Oh my God..."

"Is that a yes?" he asked, smiling.

Kate squealed with delight and jumped on him, legs wrapping around his waist as her arms wrapped around his neck. She nailed him with a white-hot kiss.

And Eric's thriller became a love story.

45.

Kate bopped through the beach house, a ball of giddy, elated energy. She had Eric by the hand, pulling him excitedly toward the bedroom.

"God, we gotta pack!" she said. "What should I bring?"

"We'll buy new stuff when we get there," he told her. "Let's just go…"

"God, you're a nut!" Kate kissed him in the bedroom doorway. "Lemme just pull together a few things!" She kissed him again and headed off to the bathroom. As she did Eric smiled… then sagged against the wall.

Again he felt light-headed. Something was wrong. Eric felt hollow, his skin sweat-sheened and raw. It felt as if the very walls of the room were rejecting him. It took every ounce of strength in his being for Eric to remain standing, awake, in this place.

"Don't faint," he muttered. "Don't pass out…"

The rush passed again. Eric shook off the feeling, called out.

"Hurry, hon!" he said.

46.

Eric and Kate zoomed down PCH in Matt Black's cool car, effortlessly cutting through traffic on the snaking road. They were heading for LAX, and escape.

Kate looked out the passenger seat window, cheerfully oblivious. Eric watched the road, desperately focusing and determined. As he shifted and punched the gas he glanced in the rearview, saw a black SUV several cars back. Headlights on, windows dark tinted. It swerved menacingly, moving into the other lane; as it did a second SUV suddenly roared up behind it as the first one went into flanking position.

BAM! The second SUV pulled up behind them, nudged Eric's bumper. The car fishtailed and Eric counter-steered, gunning it harder.

"Eric what's happening?" Kate cried, instantly freaking. BAM! The SUV hit them again.

"Stop," Eric hissed at his pursuers. But the black SUV just growled and smacked them yet again. BAM!

"Goddammit, I said stop!"

But the SUV behind just hit them again: BAM! The first one loomed mere feet away, blocking them into the passing lane. Eric glanced over, saw the backseat diver's window sliding down, a gun muzzle starting to nose out.

"Hang on!" he cried.

Eric frantically downshifted, the NSX's tach redlining. An intersection was dead ahead: he saw a big rig pulling across the oncoming lane, blocking them. The second SUV howled up behind, collision imminent. Then Eric up-shifted and gunned it, squeezing through the intersection gap at ninety per and causing a massive pileup in his wake, the second SUV trash-compacting into the big rig's trailer and sending up a cinematically glorious fireball as the first fishtailed and flipped sideways, end over end over end…

…and Eric and Kate just drove.

47.

The NSX sliced through the Santa Monica tunnel, heading for the 10 and the 405 to LAX. In the opposing lanes a pair of police cruisers whooped past, heading for the pileup. Kate was freaking.

"Jesus, Eric, who were those people?" she asked. "Why were they chasing us?"

"I don't know," Eric replied, eyeballing the road. "I didn't write them." He was freaking, too, but for entirely different reasons.

"What?" she said. "I don't understand..."

"The dream you had," he urgently tried to explain. "The water... me calling your name..."

"Eric you're scaring me..."

He grabbed her hand, white-knuckle tight. "Do you remember the pier?" he asked. For a moment she met his gaze...

...and as he looked into her eyes he saw something dawning: dreamlike flashes of black churning surf... pylons looming overhead... a rushing wave...

"Eric..."

"Remember the night I told you about my movie?" he pressed on, "I don't know how but we're really in it now. But I didn't write this!"

"Stop!" she cried. "Stop it!"

Kate burst into tears then, like something was breaking inside her. She buried her face in her hands. Eric felt suddenly brutal and cruel... but strangely, intensely alive, every cell of his being alert and present. Her pain galvanized him, made him all the more determined to save her, to save them both.

"It's gonna be okay," he said, reaching out to stroke her hair. "I swear it will.

"We've just got to get away."

48.

The rest of the way to the airport Eric explained, as best he could, the strange occurrence of scriptworld, and their stranger place within it, and the odd choreography of their ever coming together at all. At a certain point Kate stopped crying: she just listened, taking it all in, but whether it was acceptance or shock, Eric couldn't say. She nodded at some points and softly shook her head at others, but her eyes remained fixed on some distant point, as if seeing beyond the horizon. At a certain point her hands went demurely to her lap, touching and twisting the engagement ring over and over on her finger. Watching her was like watching Elizabeth Kubler Ross's five stages of dying grief model — denial, anger, bargaining, depression, acceptance — play out in real time shadow form across her face.

When he reached the point in the telling of that last night on the pier, Eric tread very lightly. He knew she didn't want to go there in her mind, which was fine with him. He didn't want to, either.

And he knew somehow he needed to stay here: in this moment, in this now. Eric bit back his own panic, fought the worry that if he let down his guard, dropped the vigilance, something bad would happen.

"I don't understand," Kate said at last. "If you created all this, why can't you just change it?"

"I don't know," Eric said. They were off the freeway now and driving down the boulevard towards LAX, the cluttered hodgepodge of taco stands, strip joints, billboards, long term parking signs and hotel chains whipping by. "It came to life and now it's alive, and it has a mind of its own..." he continued, the stoplights turning green because he willed them green. "Some things I can control, others..." Eric downshifted and gunned around a FedEx truck. "I don't know..."

They arrived at LAX and Eric steered into the parking structure at the Tom Bradley International Terminal. He found the first empty slot and pulled in. He looked around wildly as they climbed out of the car; Kate picked up on his paranoia.

"Where are we going?" she asked.

"Someplace far way," Eric said. "Somewhere the story's never been."

"Won't they follow us?"

Eric paused, gave her a grim smile.

"Not on Marty's budget," he said.

He grabbed her hand and together they ran for the terminal.

49.

They got about fifty feet when they heard the rumble of V-8s gunning up, and the two black SUVs suddenly appeared in front of and behind them, boxing them in. The same ones that had crashed on PCH. The same ones from the parking garage scene, and the firefight there. The door opened and the same menacing goons piled out, rushing them.

But I killed you! Eric thought madly. I killed you all!

This alas did not seem to hinder them. Eric let go of Kate's hand and howled with rage, laying into them, fighting for their lives.

But he was not Matt Black now, just middle-aged Eric. And the men promptly kicked the living shit out of him with fists and knees and feet and gun butts. It was eight on one, and Eric didn't stand a chance.

"KATE!!!!" he screamed, as he landed in a heap on the concrete. He blinked back blood and caught glimpse of her being grabbed and strong-armed into the back of one of the trucks. A goon piled in after her, slammed the door, and the truck roared away.

"KATE!!!!!"

Just then Eric looked up to see a well-aimed boot coming straight for his head.

It connected with a skull-crunching thump. Eric saw galaxies pinwheel and flare, and then blackness.

And just like that, he was out.

50.

The next thing Eric knew he was sprawled — battered, bruised and bloodied — on the floor of his office. He came to, aching and groaning. His vision blurred and spun. Something was blinking in the swirling mind fog. Eric focused, saw it clearly. His answering machine.

He crawled over to the edge of his desk, reached up and hit the play button. The message dutifully played.

"Eric this is Nick," Nick's voice was chilly, stiff. "I got a very disturbing call from Martin Blumenthal's office. It wasn't easy but I talked Marty out of killing the project outright, but they've decided to go another way." A chill pause. "You're out, Eric. They got another writer in. I'm sorry."

The message beeped off. Eric was dazed and dumbstruck — not that he was fired, apart from the gallows-drop freefall feeling of such news it would be stupid to think he wasn't after his little meltdown. It was the last bit of Nick's message that made Eric's blood run cold.

They got another writer in…

"Oh fuck," he gasped.

51.

Eric hauled ass up the freeway, a Bluetooth headset crammed in one ear, his defunct HOOYAH! I.D. hanging from its lanyard on the rearview mirror. It had taken ten calls to get through to Nick but he finally did — now he was plainly beseeching, any pretense of tinseltown cool having fled him utterly.

"Nick, you gotta get them to hire me back," he begged. "Tell Marty I'll pay for the fuckin' window. I'll be good, I swear..."

"Eric..." Nick drew his name out with practiced aggrieve. "If you had a recent hit under your belt you could have driven Marty's Porsche into his pool after you fucked his undocumented au pair. But I'm sorry buddy, nobody wants to deal with a "problem" writer these days ..."

"But I know how to fix this, Nick!" Eric countered. "I just need another chance..."

From the other end, silence. He was heading through the hills. "Hello?" he said into the headset. "Hello??"

But the call — like his career — had just gone dead.

Il Tratorria was a modestly hip little eatery in the shadow of the studio — low-priced Italian, shitty parking, a brisk walk from the Burbank lot. The lunch crowd was heavy on development execs hustling mid-level meetings, but Marty had been known to slum there for a quick nosh when there wasn't someone he wanted to impress.

Eric hovered outside, chain-smoking — unshaven, disheveled, looking more than a little crazed. He peered through the window, caught a glimpse through the crowd of Marty's assistant Todd, waiting at a table. Martin was there too: Eric watched as he got up to use the bathroom. As he did Eric waved at Todd; Todd glanced up and saw Eric, looked visibly alarmed.

Todd said something to the young waitress and eased his way out, smiling; but as he emerged, his vibe went hushed and urgent.

"Jesus what happened to you?" he asked.

"Nothing," Eric said. "I got in a fight…"

"What the fuck are you doing here Eric? Marty'll shit if he sees you!"

Eric had always liked Todd: he was young and maybe two years to the town, from somewhere in Central Pennsylvania. He had a pretty wife and a one bedroom apartment in Studio City, wanted to act and would do well in this town, but hadn't been in the biz long enough yet to have his entire soul scraped off.

"Todd you gotta get me back in," Eric said. "I know how to fix this…"

"No way man, I'm not getting fired for you," Todd exclaimed, lighting a smoke and blowing a harsh plume. "Christ, you're barred from the lot!"

They glanced back at the studio, looming like a plush walled fortress. "There's got to be a way…" Eric said.

"Forget about it," Todd replied, shaking his head. "Besides, the studio brought another writer in. They're changing everything…"

"But Turnaround is mine!"

"It's not 'Turnaround' anymore!" Todd told him. "It's called 'The Demon Hole' now: psychic P.I. on the trail of a mysterious woman possessed by a computer-based demon. She devours men with her vagina dentata… God, I hate this fucking town!"

Todd stubbed his smoke. "I gotta go," he said, turning to leave. Eric was frantic.

"But if Nick talks to Marty…" he began.

Todd turned, exasperated. "Don't you get it?" he said. "Who do you think the new writer's agent is?"

It clicked into place in a heartbeat. Not a surprise. But Eric felt the noose tightening, just the same. "What can I do?" he asked.

Todd paused at the door, resigned and cynical.

"Hey, you're still first writer," he said. "It gets made, you get paid."

52.

Eric was back in scriptworld, but it all felt wrong: like he was a stranger in his own dream world. He came back to find himself as himself: plain old Eric, disheveled and distraught, standing at the ocean's edge as the last rays of sun kissed the Pacific, waves splashing up to soak his clothes. There was no one else on the beach; indeed, no one as far as he could see. No cars on the road, either. And as the sun sank over the horizon he saw no lights in any of the houses lining the water, save one, far in the distance up the coast. A solitary twinkling, in an ever darkening world.

Eric started walking, as dusk fell and gave way to night. And as he got closer, he recognized it. The beach house.

Eric staggered up the cobblestone drive, winded and more ragged than ever. A marine layer had drifted in, swathing the house in mist. The light from the windows was not warm and welcoming but rather, cold and foreboding. The NSX and the Jag were parked in the driveway courtyard. Eric went to the front door, tried it. Locked.

He knocked. No answer. Eric knocked harder, fist pounding burnished oak.

The door cracked open. Toad was there, looking fiercer than ever. He glared at Eric.

"Yeah?"

"Toad, it's me," Eric said. "Lemme in…"

He tried to push past but Toad's meaty hand landed on his chest, pushing him back. "Who the fuck're you?" he snarled.

Just then someone appeared behind Toad, backlit in the cold

glow of the doorway. As he stepped forward Eric saw Matt Black in the flesh — looking altogether a younger, sleeker, stronger version of Eric, with a double-dose of pure hardass nastiness, to boot.

"Who is it?" Black asked.

"Fuckin' bum," Toad sniffed, seeing nothing else.

"Get rid of 'im."

And with that Toad grabbed Eric by the shirt, manhandling him up the drive toward the street. Eric flailed and struggled to no avail; Toad was too big, too strong, armed, and in no mood.

Toad dragged Eric to the drive's edge, pushed him out, off the property. Eric stumbled, fell, came up. As he did he saw Matt Black exiting with a beautiful blonde in tow. Eric recognized her.

"Kate!!!" he called out.

Back in the drive, Kate gazed in his direction — she looked exotic, hard like the rest of them. Cold. But as she paused near the cars something crossed her perfectly made-up face — a faint glimmer of recognition, and confusion.

"Eric...?" Kate suddenly murmured, strange thoughts flitting across her too-perfect features.

It was then that Black grabbed her, strong-arming her toward the car.

"Shut up," he said to her. "Get in..."

He tried to muscle her; Kate pulled away, memory dawning. Suddenly she cried out.

"Eric!!!"

Back in the drive, Eric struggled with Toad, punching him hard in his pocked and gnarly face. Toad took it and came back, wrapping Eric in a spine-crushing bear hug. Eric fumbled and reached for Toad's shoulder holster slung under the big man's left arm, going for the gun. As he did Toad dropped Eric, grabbed his collar and punched him hard in the solar plexus — once, twice, three times — in rapid succession.

Eric sucked hard wind and fell back, landing with a crash...

...and the next Eric knew he was laying fetal on the living room floor of his apartment back at the Seascape Apartments. He was battered, beaten, alone.

But as he scrabbled to his feet he realized: he was holding Toad's gun in his hand. He shoved into his jacket pocket and looked around wildly. He was not entirely sure how long he'd been gone this time, but it was clear enough, Paige had been there in his absence. As evidenced by the absence of pretty much everything in the apartment.

The living room was empty. Bedroom, empty. Kitchen, bathroom, bare. And his office — well, everything material had been stripped from his world, including his bookshelves, his papers, his desk…

…but laying on the floor where his desk had been, his laptop. Almost like an insult. Eric flicked the light switch. The power was off. But the laptop's screen was glowing.

"Oh no…" Eric scooped it up. "How much?"

He saw the battery meter drop from 70% to 69%. Eric looked around the empty room. No charger.

"Shit!"

53.

Ten minutes later Eric entered Mo Jo Rising, a little coffee joint just off the main drag. He looked crazed and intense as he pressed past the inevitable clot of yuppies, hipsters, and pseudo-intellectuals sipping pricey java and toodling on their laptops and iPads, beelining for the sole empty table in sight. As he sat he cut off a snotty soccer mom; she gauged his appearance, found him unworthy.

"Excuse me," she began.

"You're excused," he said, and sat at the table. Soccer mom huffed but decided perhaps best not to pursue it further. As she retreated Eric opened the laptop, checked the power level. It read 65%. Not good.

"I opened this door," he murmured. "I can bloody well close it…"

Eric took his seat, readying himself to the task. Then he started erasing Kate —scene by scene, line by line — from the script.

54.

Eric wrote and re-wrote feverishly, racing against time as the battery meter inexorably sank. He had bought a large coffee to secure his stay; it sat untouched as his fingers played across the keys. The place had largely cleared out, but he had been there too long, was putting out too much weird, intense vibe. A young barista girl had been pointedly bussing empty tables all around him, hoping he might get the hint. Finally, she approached.

"Sir?" she began. She was young and lithe, with multiple piercings and a name tag that read SARAH. "Sir, we're closing up now..."

Katie stood her ground. "Sir, please..."

Eric looked at the power meter, saw it drop from 20% to 19%. "Fuck," he hissed. He kept typing.

"Sir..."

"Sarah I understand but could you please just back off??" Eric snarled.

He looked up. Sarah had company.

The next thing Eric knew he was being rousted by two beefy Hispanic dishwashers, who bum-rushed him to the door. As the first one pushed him out the second shoved the laptop onto his arms. Eric caught it, then fumbled and it slipped from his grasp, banging onto the sidewalk.

"No!!" he cried. "You assholes!!"

"Fuck off, pendejo!" the second dishwasher called back. They locked the front door behind him, laughing.

Eric hunkered near the dumpster in the rear parking lot, cradling the laptop between his knees, assessing the damage. The case was cracked and the display glitched, and as it powered up it made a worrisome clicking sound. But it booted.

Eric opened the file, nervously watching as the power meter read 7%...6%...

"C'mon, c'mon," he muttered. The file opened. He wrote madly, laying in the last words. Finally he typed:

And together they zoom off into a perfect California night. FADE TO BLACK. ROLL CREDITS. END.

"Yes!" He smiled triumphantly. Suddenly he heard a little ding and the screen dimmed. A dialogue box appeared on the screen: Warning, You Are Now Running On Reserve Power...

"No!" Eric gasped. He scrambled to email the script. There was no Wi-Fi signal.

"Fuck!" The power meter was down to 3%. Eric fumbled in his jacket pocket, pulled out the flash drive and plugged it in, desperately copying the file. As it did the power meter sank to 3%...2%...

The screen went black.

"Fuck!!!!"

He stood, holding the computer in quivering hands. He wanted to shake it like an Etch-A-Sketch, to smash it against the wall. It was just a high tech paperweight now. Eric unplugged the little flash drive. Behind him the coffee shop's lights went out, bathing him in shadow.

Eric crossed to the far side of the lot and his car, dropped the useless laptop on the passenger seat and climbed in. As he did he felt something pinch into his side, reached into his jacket pocket. Toad's gun. He dropped that on the seat, too.

He was utterly screwed. Eric sighed grievously as all hope fled him. He closed his eyes and leaned back into the headrest. It was over. He'd blown it. There was no hope at all. He wondered if Toad's gun actually worked. That would be convenient.

If only... he thought. If only...

Eric opened his eyes, caught glimpse of himself in the

rearview mirror. An infinitely tired and haggard gaze stared back. He fished the flash drive out of his pocket, held it in his palm. As he did his gaze flitted to the gun, the dangling I.D. hanging from the rearview. Eric looked back at his reflection, saw a mad thought spark in those exhausted eyes.

Then he smiled, completely crazed, at his one last brilliant, impossible, utterly stupid idea.

55.

Sneaking into HOOYAH! was not nearly as difficult as imagined: it was the graveyard shift and a skeletal staff, the hallways pretty much deserted, the SEO section low-lit, lights of monitors glowing like the lights of a distant digital city. A few dozen workers were scattered across the vast space, each lost in their own private world. Eric wore his lanyard and acted like he was supposed to be there. But no one was really paying attention.

He reached his old workstation, sat in the Aeron chair, tried to log in. No go. He tried again, offering alternate passwords. The computer dinged — Access Denied.

"Shit," he hissed. "Shit…"

He was locked out of the system. They'd nuked his identity.

Eric was desperately seeking a workaround when Gillian came down the hall, heading home for the night. She glanced over and saw him, approached warily.

"Eric, what are you doing here?" she said, hushed.

"I just need two minutes, Gillian," Eric pleaded. "Then I'm gone forever, I swear…"

"You can't be here!" she told him. "Christ, I could get fired!"

"Gillian, please," Eric pressed, voice rising. "Just log me in…"

Around them, heads started to peer up from their screens, the drama penetrating their stillness. One simpering little perm employee — his nametag read DWIGHT — got up from his desk, came over.

"Everything okay, Gill?" he asked.

Gillian looked from Eric to Dwight, stepped away. "He's not

supposed to be here," she told him. "Call Security..."

Dwight nodded and hustled away, feeling manly and empowered. And that was when Eric jumped up.

"NO!" he roared, then reached into his jacket and pulled out Toad's big gun. Eric waved it menacingly. "Everyone out! NOW!!"

The night shift alternately froze and scrambled — most fleeing but some caught in deer-in-the-headlights shock. At least two whipped out their cam phones, YouTube joining fight-or-flight as an instinctive 21st century reaction. Eric pulled the trigger on the gun: BLAM! BLAM! BLAM! Ear-shatteringly loud and with a blazing muzzle flash. Toad's gun worked, after all... but even more, like a movie gun, enhanced for effect. It sounded like a freaking howitzer. He had aimed it at the ceiling. As the gerbils fled the hi-tech cage he was perhaps the only one who noticed: there were no bullet holes there.

Eric followed as the last of the perms cleared the big double-doors. He locked them and pushed a desk in front of them, blocking entry, playing disgruntled-ex-employee-gone-postal to the hilt.

"GET THE FUCK OUT!!" he cried. ANYONE COMES IN HERE AND..."

BLAM! BLAM! BLAM! BLAM! Eric fired for punctuation and effect, then cackled madly.

"BWAHAHAAHAH, ARE WE HAVING FUN YET????"

From the other side, silence. Victory was fleetingly his. But as he headed for a freshly abandoned workstation, he could hear the distant wail.

Police sirens.

56.

The sirens outside grew louder; Eric could see red and blue lights reflecting off the building facades as he made his way across the floor. He peered out one window and saw the entire street cordoned off, easily two dozen patrol units blocking access. Plus news vans and the big black boxy truck emblazoned SWAT. From above a searchlight swept down across the windows. LAPD chopper. He caught glimpse of two other choppers slicing through the night sky. TV news crews.

Ducking deep inside, Eric found a logged-in workstation. He sat and plugged the flash drive into the CPU, waited for the icon to appear on the digital desktop. It was a perm station and thus festooned with toys and geek memorabilia: a little plastic SpongeBob Squarepants grinned up at him from the desk, flanked by many tiny leering Freddy Kruegers and hockey-masked Jason Voorhees posed in an impromptu conga line.

The icon popped up on the screen. Suddenly an authoritative voice called out from the other side of the barricaded doors.

"THIS IS THE LAPD! DROP YOUR WEAPON AND COME OUT WITH YOUR HANDS UP!!"

Out in the hall, Gillian hung back by the elevators with uniformed officers as a dozen black-clad, body armored and heavily armed men clustered near the door. They were strapped with enough ordnance to invade a small country. The lead officer spoke into his comm set, communicating with the ASD unit hovering outside.

"Air, do you have a visual?" he asked.

"Negative," the chopper pilot crackled back. "He's too deep in…"

As they readied themselves for entry they suddenly heard Eric calling back from the other side of the door.

"I'VE GOT A HOSTAGE!!" he cried.

Back on the SEO floor Eric hunkered near the door, Toad's gun in one hand, SpongeBob in the other. "ANYONE COMES IN," he threatened, "AND 'BOB' GETS IT!!"

Back at the Seascape Apartments it was a slow night. Marin kicked back in her bunny slippers and poured a fresh glass of box wine from the fridge as Bob took a massive toke off his bong. The TV was playing in a corner of the crowded room: on the screen a vertiginous Action Skycam visual popped up, a garish chevron beneath: LIVE: INTERNET TERRORIST ATTACK?

"Whoa," Bob husked through a lungful of sweet ganja smoke.

Back in the hallway Gillian came out of her office with a printout and news: no Bob, Robert, Rob on staff. She also had Eric's employee file, and the location of exactly which computer was active on the floor. She handed it to a detective who took it to the SWAT team leader; he nodded to the others, who readied a battering ram, gas masks and flash bang grenades.

"THIS IS YOUR LAST WARNING!" The lead SWAT called out. No answer. He looked at his men, signaled GO.

In his remaining mortal seconds Eric scrambled back to the workstation, hit send on the email. He watched frantically as the file transfer bar read 50%...60%...70%...

"Fuck, c'mon!" he growled.

As it reached 90% he grasped the flash drive in his fingers. "Please," he murmured. "Please…"

…and in the last two seconds Time skewed once again, as Eric heard a series of sharp pops, the cops cutting the power and the lights going off in sections — POP! POP! POP! POP! The digital landscape before him blacked out as it moved closer and closer…

…and SWAT rammed the blocked door and tossed in flash-bang grenades.

Pa-POW! Pa-POW! Pa-POW!

The last thing Eric saw was the whole floor searing with blinding smoke and light.

57.

"Whoa, nice light show!" The LAPD chopper pilot's voice barked in the comm set. They could see it from two thousand feet. The SWAT lead came back.

"Stand by, Bravo going in..."

Thick acrid smoke swirled in the air, pierced by the laser dots from a dozen armed officers, fanning out in gas masks, searching the floor. From the section grid they knew exactly where he was supposed to be.

Over the comm sets, voices called out. Clear... clear... clear!"

As they zeroed in, they saw an Aeron chair, twisting slowly around toward them. The laser sights all zoomed in...

...but as it completed its turn they just saw the little rubber SpongeBob toy grinning up at them from the seat.

The lead SWAT lifted his gas mask, blinking back the stinging smoke. He looked around.

"He's fucking gone..." he said.

58.

It was shortly before noon when workmen finished installing the new conference room window at Martin Blumenthal Productions. Todd was in there working as Martin came in, barking into his headset to Nick the agent.

"What do you mean 'he's sick'?" he said. "I need the new draft! The studio's up my freakin' ass!"

"I'm sorry Marty," Nick pleaded. "He broke both his arms in a freak para-skiiing accident in Cabo! He's in casts from his knuckles to his neck!"

"What the fuck is he doing in Cabo when he should be writing??" Martin wailed. "The studio hates the new draft! Lindsey dropped out — she thinks the part of 'Kate' is exploitative. She can't even spell exploitative! She calls it 'expoitive'! The whole goddam project is in jeopardy!"

"What do you want me to do, Marty?" Nick asked.

"FIX it!!" Martin yowled.

He hung up, sat down at his laptop. Todd brought him coffee. Marty looked up. "Got any good news?" he asked.

"Uhm…" Todd handed him an email printout. "The Japanese investors don't like their ROI on Bloodsucking Bastards. They want to see our books…"

"Christ," Martin buried his head in his hands. As Todd exited Martin checked his email and nursed a migraine. His laptop chimed. Martin saw the incoming script from Eric.

"Oh, gimme a break," he mumbled.

Todd was back at his desk, doing his story reports when he heard Martin call out.

"Todd!"

Todd instantly jumped up, hustled in. "Yeah Marty…" he began.

Martin had his glasses pushed down his nose, staring at the laptop screen. "Get me a Motrin," he said, still reading. "And get Eric Best on the phone…"

"Eric," Todd said, taken off guard. "Why?"

But Martin just hot him a sack-shriveling gaze, and Todd dutifully retreated. Martin kept speed reading, muttering to himself. "Little bastard pulled it off…"

He called out to Todd. "You got him?" A pause. Then Todd called back.

"His phone's been disconnected!"

Marty Blumenthal lowered his head to one hand grievously. "Fucking writers…" he groaned.

59.

The funky old Cadillac tooled north on the Pacific Coast Highway, heading away from LA as a golden sun set over the ever-glittering ocean. The horizon was a rainbow pastiche of hues, the many shades blue, gold, amber, orange, and yellow all melding together gloriously.

The Caddie's top was down. Eric was behind the wheel. The wind didn't whip his cropped and thinning hair, but he looked tanned, rested, clad in loose linen jacket, white cotton shirt, and jeans. The weather was pristine. PCH dipped and looped before him.

Eric caught glimpse of his eyes in the rearview. The only bags he had were stowed neatly in the Caddie's trunk. He was finally at peace with himself, and the world.

Or more to the point, his scriptworld.

Everyone's the star of their own movie, Gabe had told him once. Don't let yourself become a supporting player in someone else's drama.

Yeah but how does that work in real life? Eric had asked. What do you do when your life is a movie but you hate it?

Re-write it? Gabe had offered.

And so he did. Not by making himself a star, or even a supporting player. Not even a day player. More like, an extra. A mere face in the crowd: there for a moment, then gone.

And the show, as they say, went on.

Your script, Marty had warned. My fucking movie...

Yup, Eric now thought to himself. And this one's mine...

He looked over at Kate, one bare foot propped upon in the wide dash. She wore a short denim jacket, a sheer summer dress and three little silver toe rings on her tan and sandaled feet. The toe rings glinted in the warm golden light. Her head was tilted back into the seat rest, eyes closed. She looked relaxed and happy — no longer haunted, just casually, serenely beautiful. She opened her eyes and caught Eric looking at her. Kate reached out and took his hand.

"How you doin'?" he asked.

"Good," she replied. "Great." She smiled, and then a brief, furtive shadow flitted across her features.

"What?" he asked. She paused for a moment, pensive.

"Will we be okay?" she asked him hesitantly.

"We will," Eric answered. "We already are."

"Where do we go now?"

"Wherever we want," Eric said. "We're free, babe..."

Kate smiled. Paused again.

"Where is it?" she asked, almost as if afraid to hear the answer. "The script..."

Eric squeezed her hand, gazed out at the fat and setting sun. "Someplace they'll never find it," he told her.

He flashed her a confident grin, then glanced at his keychain, dangling from the ignition. The flash drive was hanging from it.

A hundred yards ahead, an eighteen-wheeler made a left turn into the southbound lane at the intersection, chugging up the hill. As it passed Eric unclipped the flash drive from the key ring, winked at her, and tossed it out the open window.

The big rig's tires crunched it underneath, flattening it to a cracked little plastic and silicon pancake. Eric watched in the rearview as the truck lumbered on, unheeding.

Kate whooped with glee and slid over, wrapping her arms around his neck. Up ahead, the intersection light turned red. Eric nodded to it.

"Whaddaya say? A road we've never been down before?"

"Go for it," she replied, snuggling up to him on the seat.

Eric hit the gas. As the speedometer climbed he squinted at the traffic light. It turned green just as they got there. Kate whooped again, fisting the sky as the Caddie rolled on through.

And together they zoomed off into a perfect California night.

FADE UP ON:

It was almost seven p.m. as Todd sat at his desk, trying to wrap his work for the day. He had a seven-thirty drinks meeting over the hill at Barney's Beanery on Santa Monica, an indie producer who'd seen his reel and wanted to talk about a part. Some low-budget horror flick destined to go straight to DVD and streaming on the Net, but a part was a part. Todd looked at the clock. Cutting it close.

He wrote TURNAROUND on the spine of Eric's script with a black Sharpie. Just then the phone rang.

"Martin Blumenthal's office," he answered into his headset, listened. "I'm sorry Nick, he's on a call right now, can I have him ring you back?" Listening more. "Yes, I think he's talking to him right now… okay, I will."

Todd rang off and put Eric's script with a pile of other drafts, then grabbed some papers needing signature. As he did he glanced at his LCD monitor: the HOOYAH! News splash page was up. Eric's employee photo was there, with the banner Search For Terror Writer Continues!

Todd left his little office and continued down the hall to Marty's more spacious digs: as he entered Marty was tilted back in a two thousand dollar memory foam Relax the Back desk chair, chatting into the speakerphone as he gazed out the windows at the fading LA sky. Todd dutifully place the signature papers on Marty's desk and moved away with the pile of scripts. Marty signed and kept talking.

"So anyway, I read your sample that Nick sent over and what can I say, I'm a huge fan," Marty effused. "I'd like to get started on this ASAP…"

Todd walked past the dry-wipe project board, where a pretty new intern was erasing The Demon Hole from the development list. He placed Eric's scripts in a tall bookshelf, flanked by dozens of other scripts. All defunct shots at former celluloid glory. All now residing, moldering and forgotten, in the turnaround pile.

Todd showed his watch and mouthed to Marty, gotta go. Marty nodded and waved him off; Todd collected the signed papers and beat a hasty retreat.

"Hey, what about the other movie you were doing, the one with whatsisname —?" The new writer's voice was tinny over the speaker phone. "The nut who blew up HOOYAH!? God what a freak…"

"It's history, forget about it," Marty said, looking at the pretty intern's ass. He smiled winningly.

"Let's talk about you."

ABOUT THE AUTHOR

CRAIG SPECTOR is an award-winning and bestselling author, editor, and screenwriter, with twelve books published, reprints in nine languages, and millions of copies in print. His fiction has been published by Tor Books/St. Martins Press, Bantam Books, Harper Collins, Pocket Books, Arbor House, Crossroad Press, and others; his film and television work includes projects for TNC Pictures, Anonymous Content, ABC, NBC, Fox Television, Hearst Entertainment, Davis Entertainment Television, New Line Cinema, Beacon Pictures, Wonderful World of Disney, and others.

An accomplished musician and graduate of the Berklee College of Music [1982], Spector released an album of original music in 2017, CRAIG SPECTOR: RESURRECTION ROAD, chronicling his ongoing journey fighting Stage Four metastatic prostate cancer; it was followed in 2018 by a second album, OUTPOSTS, and in 2019, KICKING CANS, the third in his Art of Not Dying cycle. You can find more info on his music at www.craigspectormsuic.com.

Spector's first short fiction collection is currently in progress, as well as editing a freedom-of-speech themed dark fiction anthology titled FREEDOM OF SCREECH.

Curious about other Crossroad Press books?
Stop by our site:
http://store.crossroadpress.com
We offer quality writing
in digital, audio, and print formats.

Enter the code FIRSTBOOK
to get 20% off your first order from our store!
Stop by today!